COWBOY BLIND DATE MIX-UP FOR CHRISTMAS

A Very Country Christmas Wish #3

JO GRAFFORD

CONTENTS

ACKNOWLEDGMENTS

A huge thank you to my editor, Cathleen Weaver, and my beta readers — Mahasani and Pigchevy — for helping me make this sweet Christmas romance story the best it can be. I also want to give a shout out to my Cuppa Jo Readers on Facebook. Thank you for reading and loving my books!

CHAPTER 1: BLIND DATE MISTAKE

CHRISTIE

Why did I let her talk me into this?

Christie Hart tried to resist the temptation to glance at her watch again. And failed. There was no point in denying the truth any longer. It was a full fifteen minutes past six o'clock, the pre-agreed time for meeting her blind date at the sandwich shop.

Or holi-date as her boss and good friend, Willa Castellano, insisted on calling it. *Absolutely no questions! It's a surprise,* she'd said.

Well, she was right about that. Being stood up by a man Christie had never laid eyes on was certainly a surprise. Just not a good one.

Shivering in the mountain breeze, she inwardly debated what to do next. She was standing outside The Gingerbread House, a cozy little sandwich and coffee bistro in Pinetop, Arizona. Up and down Main Street, store windows twinkled with Christmas lights, even the shops that were closed for the evening. The street lights were glinting with metallic holiday garlands in a variety of shapes — angels, bells, candy canes, and pine trees.

"Ho! Ho! Ho! Come on in and watch the fudge show." A man dressed as Santa paced in front of The North Pole Candy Depot two doors down. He was handing out coupons to every passer-by who stopped to peer inside the display window. On the other side of the glass, candy makers in red and white striped hats were pushing a fresh batch of fudge back and forth across a marble slab with their long-handled paddles. The warm chocolate slowly cooled and would eventually be twirled and paddled into the shape of their choice.

The front door of the shop opened, and a laughing couple stepped onto the sidewalk. The scent of fudge swirled out the door with them, caught on the breeze, and wafted Christie's way.

Her stomach growled in response, reminding her that she'd skipped lunch to save enough calories for dessert this evening.

During a date that clearly isn't going to happen.

Any sane, self-respecting woman would call it a night and head home in disgust. Apparently, her would-be blind date had gotten cold feet. Or become ill. Or been chased down the mountain by a bear.

She swallowed a chuckle at the mental image her brain conjured up of a man running from a bear. Blowing out a frosty breath of resignation, she turned away from the entrance of The Gingerbread House. So much for pulling the tags off the new black velvet pants she'd ordered from a clothing boutique in New York! She'd paired them with hand-tooled custom cowgirl boots. Their four-inch heels were every bit as daring as the stunts she performed. It was too bad there was no special guy in her life to see her in them tonight.

As she took the first step toward her car, her cell phone rang. It was no normal ring, either. It was the custom ringtone Willa had insisted on installing for herself on Christie's phone — a comically annoying, nasally voice that demanded, "Answer me! Answer me! Answer me right now, giiiirl!"

Blushing with embarrassment, she hastily unzipped her purse and fished around for the phone, whose volume she'd forgotten to turn down before leaving the house.

She was chuckling helplessly by the time she lifted it to her ear and connected the line. "You're killing me, Willa! That's the most ridiculous ringtone on the planet."

"I know, right?" Her friend's voice held zero guilt. "Listen, I am soooo sorry, but there's been a terrible mix-up with your blind date."

"Oh, I am well aware." Christie's voice was dry. "But, hey! I got to experience something new tonight since I've never been stood up on a date before." Not that she went on many dates.

She glanced longingly toward the candy shop as another sickeningly happy couple emerged hand-in-hand. Maybe she'd skip dinner altogether and treat herself to a piece of consolation fudge on the way home.

"No, sweetie! That's not what's going on at all." Willa sounded a little harried. "Where exactly are you? Because neither of your dates have seen hide or hair of you yet."

"Neither?" Christie choked out a cough as she spun back toward the entrance of The Gingerbread House. "You say that like there's more than one."

"Yeah," Willa sighed. "That's the mix-up I was talking about. I don't know how it happened or whose fault it is. Maybe I got my wires crossed with one of them. All I know for sure is that two guys are waiting inside the bistro for you as we speak."

"You're kidding," Christie moaned. "Please tell me you're kidding."

Willa continued speaking as if she hadn't heard her. "Where did you say you're at?"

I didn't say. "Outside." Christie clenched her teeth to keep them from chattering. She glanced around her, half-tempted to make a run for her Jeep before her disastrous evening got any worse.

"You must be freezing," Willa gasped.

Among other things. Christie cast another longing look at the candy shop. She was so hungry by now that she would happily start chewing on one of the stirring paddles.

"Go inside right now," her friend ordered. "We'll sort this out, I promise."

"Willa!" Christie couldn't believe she was acting like it was no big deal. "There's no way you can expect me to sit across the table from not one but two men I've never met before." Her voice rose to a trilling note of indignation. She couldn't begin to imagine how awkward that would be.

"I don't. Of course, I don't expect that, sweetie!" Willa gave a breathy chuckle. "Just go inside and pick one of them to have dinner with tonight. You can reschedule with the other one later. I've already explained to both of them what's going on and apologized profusely. They're great guys, and they're being really cool about it. I promise."

"Pick one of them, huh?" Christie huffed out a laugh, unable to believe what she was hearing. "I'm sort of dying out here on the sidewalk at the mere thought of—no." She shook her head. "I can't do it. Just...no."

"Yes, you can, sweetie. We had a deal." Her friend's voice turned wheedling.

By deal, she was referring to the fact that Christie had lost two out of three rounds of rock-paper-scissors a few nights ago over a dare she should've never accepted in the first place.

"You caught me in a weak moment," she protested. "I was training with my horse all afternoon. I was too tired to think straight."

"That's kind of what tonight is all about," Willa reminded. "We agreed that you work too hard and need to get out more. You promised you would keep an open mind about this."

"Well, I'm hereby exercising my right to change my mind. It's too much pressure." Christie pressed a hand to her heart, trying to get a grip on her runaway stress level. It was crazy how she could calmly perform all sorts of daring stunts on the back of her horse. But send her on a blind date, and she was about to go into cardiac arrest. *Correction. Make that two blind dates.*

The door to the sandwich bistro swung open, and a tall, dark-haired cowboy stepped outside to join her on the sidewalk. "Hey, Christie! I'm Wes." Amusement thickened his voice as he thrust a gloved hand in her direction. "Wes Wakefield."

Wes Wakefield? As in Bonnie's Wes? The familiar name turned her knees to jelly. It had been like six or seven years since the last time she'd laid eyes on her college roomie's smoking hot stepbrother. Then again, maybe there was more than one Wes Wakefield in the world. It wasn't an overly common name, but...

"I, er..." She stared at his outstretched hand for a moment. Then her gaze slowly traveled upward. Though she couldn't see his features perfectly beneath the muted glow of the streetlights, it was him alright. She'd recognize that rangy frame and squared-off chin anywhere.

Unbelievable! My blind date is Wes Dreamboat Wakefield.

One of her blind dates, anyway. For a moment, the world tilted dizzily. Stuff like this was only supposed to happen in the movies, not in the middle of remote little mountain towns like Pinetop, Arizona.

And don't even get her started on the fact that blind dates were supposed to be with people you didn't know, right?

She pointed a shaky finger at her phone to let him know

she was on a call. It was way too bad he was standing close enough to hear every word she said, because she was dying to ask her boss if she had anything to do with his sudden appearance.

"Is that Wes?" Willa's voice held an element of slyness against her ear.

Christie gripped the phone harder. "I, er, how did you—?"

Willa cut her off with a squeal of excitement. "Looks like one of your holi-dates found you, so I'm going to simply hang up and let you enjoy your evening." The gushing tenor of her voice raised Christie's suspicions even further.

Pressing her lips against the mouthpiece, she hissed, "Have you been texting him the whole time you were talking to me?"

With a guilty chuckle, Willa disconnected the line.

Christie was left, gazing open-mouthed at Wes Wakefield. She could only presume her other blind date was still inside the bistro.

Waiting for me to choose who I'm going to have dinner with tonight. Christie wished the sidewalk would open and swallow her up. Unfortunately, it did not, which meant there was no escaping this.

"Hi, Wes." Her heart felt like it was banging a few hundred beats per minute as she slid her phone back into her purse. Then she reached out to clasp the hand he was still offering.

To her dismay, there wasn't a drop of recognition in his warm, dark gaze as they shook hands.

Her heart cracked a little at the realization that the man she'd been unable to forget didn't have the foggiest recollection of her in return.

He stepped closer and splayed one large hand on the small of her back to nudge her toward the door of The Gingerbread House. "It's cold out here. How about we take this conversation inside?" Though he was studying her curiously from beneath the brim of his black leather Stetson, there was still no recognition in his features.

Giving him a wobbly smile, she stepped into the building ahead of him.

Another darkly handsome cowboy in jeans and boots was speaking to a smiling hostess at the check-in podium. He pivoted in her direction as Wes continued nudging her forward.

Christie could only presume he was her second blind date. He, too, looked familiar, though she wasn't sure why.

He took one look at her and hurried forward with a hand outstretched. "Hi, Christie." He tipped his beige felt Stetson at her. "I'm Roman Rios. Not sure if you've noticed me hanging around Castellano's, but I'm their newest wrangler. Started a few days ago." His bronze skin and faint Hispanic accent told her that he had some Latino blood in him. He sounded a lot like Willa's husband, Angel Castellano, the guy who owned and operated the dinner theater they were apparently both employed at.

"No wonder you look familiar." She shook his hand, feeling inexplicably shy. Never before had she been in the presence of two men at the same time who wanted to date her. "I've been told there's been a mix-up with our, ah...dinner plans." She felt another blush rise to her cheeks. Could this get any more awkward?

"Nothing we can't solve by a good old-fashioned coin toss," Wes interjected in a smooth voice. The entire time Roman had been shaking her hand, he'd been stuck to her side like velcro.

A coin toss? Seriously? He really thought he could fix tonight's dating disaster with a simple coin toss? Part of her wanted to laugh, while the other part of her wanted to curl into a fetal position on the floor and rock hopelessly back and forth. Then again, a coin toss was probably par for the course, considering that a game of rock-paper-scissors had gotten her into this mess in the first place.

She glanced wordlessly between the two men and shivered.

Wes quickly shrugged out of his black leather jacket and draped it around the foolishly thin blue jean blazer she'd worn over her red turtleneck sweater. "Better?" He raised his eyebrows curiously at her.

It was an incredibly sweet gesture to share his jacket. So much so that she almost forgave him for failing to remember her.

She caught her lower lip between her teeth, nodding gratefully. "Thank you." They were the only two words she could muster while he was casually untucking the end of her blonde ponytail from his jacket — a jacket that was still warm from his body heat, making her feel as melty as a marshmallow toasting over an open fire.

He winked at her as he pulled a silver quarter out of the front right pocket of his jeans. His gaze flickered briefly to Roman. "Wait until I toss it. Then call heads or tails while it's in the air."

Roman nodded at Wes, then shook his head at the beaming hostess. It was one of those intimate kinds of exchanges between two people who knew each other.

The woman tossed back a handful of her shoulder-length brown hair and appeared to be trying not to laugh. She looked about the same age as Roman and shared his Latino complexion. Her hand settled on the baby bump protruding from her oversized green and white plaid shirt as her head spun in Wes's direction.

Christie followed the woman's gaze in time to see Wes position the silver quarter on his thumb and forefinger.

"Don't forget to call it," he drawled, brushing his thumb

over the face of the quarter. George Washington's metallic head was facing up.

She didn't think much of it until he raised the quarter and made a snapping movement to release it into the air. At that moment, she knew exactly who her dinner date was going to be. She'd watched enough magic tricks online to recognize when a bit of sleight of hand was in play.

"Heads!" Roman's watchful gaze followed the coin as it wobbled convincingly upward, catching the glow of the overhead lights without flipping over a single time. As the head of the coin fell back into Wes's outstretched hand, he caught it and neatly flipped it over as he slapped it onto his forearm. He did it so effortlessly that Christie imagined he'd practiced it dozens of times to get it exactly right.

Both Roman and the hostess stepped closer to peer at the coin resting on Wes's arm. Christie didn't bother. She already knew that the tails side of the coin was facing up.

A moan of defeat eased out of the waitress. "Too bad." She made a pouty face at Roman.

In response, he leaned closer to give her a hug. "How about you order me a sandwich to go, sis?"

Sis. So that was their connection.

Christie inwardly debated whether to challenge Wes on the issue and demand a re-toss, one that would give her an equal shot at sitting down to dinner with her wrangler coworker.

As opposed to enduring a meal with a guy who wasn't impressed enough with me the first time we met to even remember me.

"Sorry, man." Wes didn't sound overly regretful as he pocketed the coin. "Better luck next time."

"It's alright." Roman surveyed Christie with his hands loosely propped on his hips. "It's nice to finally meet you, Christie. Wanna give me a raincheck?"

"Of course."

Though the look he gave her was admiring, she wouldn't classify it as flirtatious. "I've enjoyed watching you ride at Castellano's."

"Thanks. It's been a welcome change of pace." She'd joined the dinner theater in June, which meant she was about to reach the six-month point of her tenure with them. Before taking the job, she'd been on the rodeo circuit. Constantly on the road. Constantly towing her horse trailer from one end of the country to the other.

"I bet." Roman rocked back on the heels of his boots, surveying her gravely. "When I first heard about Castellano's opening an indoor rodeo, I had my doubts as to how well it would go over in a town this small. Glad to say I was wrong. I'm sure landing a headliner like you has helped with its success."

"It's very kind of you to say so." She smiled shyly at him, then turned to the hostess. "You're his sister, right?"

The pregnant woman nodded, still smiling, as she reached for a pair of menus beneath the cabinet. "Or his evil, interfering twin, as he prefers to call me." She shot him an affectionate look. "Everyone else calls me Izzy."

Christie decided on the spot that she liked the woman. "When's your baby due?" She eyed Izzy's blossoming belly.

"Not until April." Izzy rolled her eyes. "I get to toddle around looking like I'm carrying a beach ball under my shirt for another four months. Yippeee!" Her tone of voice indicated she was less than excited about the prospect.

For some reason, her words caused a shadow to cross her brother's face.

"Is it your first?" Christie asked, smiling in empathy.

"Yes." A glow of excitement stained her features.

"Congratulations!" A tad bit of envy stirred beneath Christie's rib cage. At the age of twenty-seven, she was well aware of how fast her own biological clock was ticking. However, she didn't even have a serious boyfriend.

"Thanks." Izzy's voice was brisk as she glanced over at Wes. "If you and Christie will follow me, we'll finish unsnarling this whole blind date mix-up." She wrinkled her nose at her brother as she spoke, clearly disappointed that she wasn't getting to seat him at a table.

Christie followed her in silence, very much aware of Wes's hovering presence at her side as they traversed the surprisingly crowded bistro. She removed his jacket from her shoulders as they reached their booth.

It was tucked into a charming alcove that was lit by a pair of flickering wall sconces. The result was a rippling, candle-like glow that was both lovely and romantic. Or would have been if Christie's stomach hadn't been tied in a snarl of so many knots. It was good seeing Wes again after all this time. Really good. It would've been even better if he'd remembered her.

She did a rapid mental calculation and determined it had been seven years since she'd last laid eyes on the hunky cowboy mechanic. Seven years since she'd dropped out of college to pursue a career as a trick rider. At the time, she'd been really close friends with his stepsister, who'd served as her college roommate. Besties for two years, anyway. They'd lost touch after Christie had hit the road. It was something she'd always regretted.

Wes remained standing while Christie slid into her side of the booth. She glanced nervously up at him, handing his leather jacket back.

"Thanks," she murmured.

He cocked a single eyebrow at her. "All warmed up?"

She nodded as he took a seat across from her. He removed his Stetson and laid it on the black vinyl cushion to his left. His hair was exactly as she remembered it, longer on top and shorter on the sides — short enough not to leave much of a hat line. There were no grease stains on his shirt tonight. That was different from her memories of him. So was his pressed, gray button-up shirt. She'd never seen him in anything other than t-shirts or plaid before.

Izzy slid a set of menus in front of them, along with silverware rolled inside white napkins. "Can I start you off with some coffee?"

"Yes, please. What do you recommend?" Since it was Christie's first visit to The Gingerbread House, she quickly opened and scanned the beverage section of the menu. It was a full two pages, not a big surprise since they were sitting inside a sandwich and coffee bistro.

"I highly recommend the Caramel Escape with a splash of chocolate creamer. If you have a sweet tooth, I can latte it up for you."

"Yes, please. That sounds amazing." Christie flipped a page of the menu to view her sandwich options.

She listened as Wes ordered his coffee black and waited until Izzy was gone to speak. "No extra tricks when it comes to your coffee, eh?" She peeked over the top of her menu at him. "Only when you're tossing quarters into the air."

He waggled his dark eyebrows playfully at her. "I have no idea what you're talking about, Miss Hart."

Her lips twitched as she returned her attention to the menu. She wished there was some way to slow the rapid cadence of her heart. "I thought waiting to have Roman call heads or tails after the coin toss was a nice touch."

"Okay. Fine. I'm guilty of hijacking our blind date and ending the mix-up for everyone involved."

She wrinkled her nose at him. "It was hardly fair to Roman. He seems really nice."

"Yes, he's a good guy," Wes agreed in an easy tone. "They don't make 'em any finer. It's one of the reasons I did what I did." His strong jawline was edged with an evening shadow. He'd shaved earlier in the day but not right before their date.

With a wry chuckle, she peeked over the top of her menu at him again. "So, let me get this straight. You admit to edging him out of our date, while at the same time claiming you did him a favor? I'm not sure how that's supposed to make me feel."

"Flattered, I hope." He hooked one long finger over her menu to lower it a couple of inches. "I was really looking forward to spending this evening with you."

She wasn't sure if her cheeks could get any warmer. They felt like they were on fire. "But...?" she prodded, sensing there was more to the story where Roman was concerned.

Wes had yet to pick up his own menu. "Roman was widowed two years ago. Back when he was still working at Christmas Tree Farm. He's still getting over his loss."

Her insides constricted with sympathy. "That's so sad!"

"It is. From what I understand, he lost her during childbirth."

It didn't sound like Wes had known Roman at the time. She laid down her menu. "I can't imagine going through something like that." It had to have been devastating.

"Me, either." He glanced up at Izzy as she sailed back in their direction with two steaming mugs of coffee. "He'll be alright, though. Eventually. His sister is determined to help him heal."

Christie watched Izzy pause her advance to allow a customer to pass in front of her. "So, pushing him out of the house on a blind date was her idea?"

"Something like that. Though she means well, I don't think he appreciates all her recent matchmaking attempts."

Izzy arrived at their booth with their coffee and set the mugs in front of them with a flourish.

"Mmm!" Christie leaned forward to give hers an appreciative sniff. "If it tastes half as good as it smells, it'll be worth every calorie I saved up for tonight." She hadn't meant to bring up the topic of her never-ending struggle to control her weight. It had sort of just slipped out. She discreetly eyed Wes from beneath her lashes to see if he'd even noticed the comment.

He was studying her through narrowed lids.

She bit back a sigh. Yeah, it looked like he'd heard her alright. It was impossible to tell what he thought of her comment, though.

Tuning back into Izzy's endless stream of chatter, she listened to tonight's specials. The bistro's Christmas Cranberry Turkey Sandwich sounded particularly amazing with its layers of cranberry sauce and butternut squash puree. She would have sprung for it in an instant if she didn't already have a liquid version of her entire day's allotment of calories filling the mug in front of her. It would be wise to offset it with lighter fare.

Biting back a sigh, she forced herself to ask the dreaded salad question. "Is it possible to order your sandwiches in a lettuce wrap?"

"Definitely!" Izzy pointed at Christie's menu. "You can get any entrée on our sandwich menu served on wheat, rye, sour dough, flatbread, spinach wraps, tomato basil wraps, or lettuce. Lots of choices."

Wes, who'd been watching Christie's expression the entire time, chose that moment to jump back into the conversation. "Or we can order two different entrees and split them."

Izzy waved a hand to acknowledge his suggestion, smiling brightly. "Or we can do that." She turned to face Christie. "Ladies first. What can I get you?"

"Undecided." She waved at Wes. "Go ahead and take his order, while I make up my mind."

"I'll have the Christmas Cranberry Turkey Sandwich," he

announced without hesitation. "My offer's still open if you want to go halves on it, Christie."

"Thanks." Her mouth watered in anticipation of getting to sample the amazing sandwich. No way was she eating half of it, though. A bite or two would be more than enough. Maybe if she left an inch of her latte in the bottom of her mug, the calorie numbers would shake out in her favor.

She placed her much less thrilling order for a wedge salad with a light drizzle of vinaigrette.

"Good choice," Izzy announced cheerfully while she collected their menus.

As she walked away to take their orders to the kitchen staff, Christie muttered without thinking, "Liar."

Wes snorted out a laugh. He leaned her way. "It's not too late to flag her down and change our ticket to a double order of Christmas Cranberry Turkey Sandwiches."

"I can't." She shook her head regretfully. "I worked too hard to get down to this size." He might not remember the other version of her, but she did. Her latte was her one big splurge tonight, and she was drawing the line at that.

Holding her gaze, he announced quietly, "Real men can handle a few extra pounds, Christie. You were beautiful the first time we met, and you're beautiful now."

His words utterly floored her. She felt her face go white, then red again. "So, you *do* remember me!" Wondering if that was a good thing, she scanned his face for any sign of disappointment.

CHAPTER 2: THE COIN TOSS
WES

"I didn't at first." Wes was having a hard time wrapping his brain around the fact that the woman sitting in front of him was actually his stepsister's roommate from college.

For the first two years, anyway. Before she'd dropped out of the pre-law classes they'd been attending together, stopped returning phone calls, and "fell off the face of the earth." Those were his sister's exact words every time he'd asked about Christie. It kind of stung that she'd cut them out of her life without so much as a goodbye.

Now here you are.

It was truly astonishing to learn that the quiet, shy college version of her in super cute long t-shirts and yoga pants had somehow transformed herself into a world-renowned trick rider.

"You look a little shellshocked." Christie shook her head at him, looking bemused.

"I am." He gestured at her with both hands, searching for the right words to explain how it looked from his angle. "In my defense, you've changed. A lot. Your hair is longer and blonder."

Once upon a time, there'd been more honey and gold in the ponytail that swung down her back. Though she looked poster perfect in her current shade of Barbie doll blonde, he wouldn't mind seeing her in her natural color again. Now didn't feel like the time to tell her, though.

Christie's lovely blue eyes had grown hard with resignation. "You might as well say it," she declared in a flat voice. "I'm half the size I used to be."

She had to be exaggerating, because he didn't remember her having more than an extra ten to fifteen pounds on her. However, her weight was clearly a sore topic, so he let her comment slide. "You also used to wear glasses." Seriously hot, dark-rimmed ones. He wished there was a way to make her see herself through his eyes. She was all the more stunning because of the challenges she'd overcome to get to where she was now. He was having a hard time tearing his gaze away from her.

"I had LASIK surgery."

He nodded slowly, liking the fact that she sounded less defensive than before. "You wore braces back then, too."

A faint smile lit her classically oval features. "It was a retainer." She sounded surprised. "I can't believe you actually remembered that."

"What can I say?" He spread his hands. "You're a memorable woman, then and now." He'd always been fascinated by her quiet intelligence, not that he'd ever acted on that interest. His stepsister had been all too quick to remind him that he was too old for her friends.

She rolled her eyes. "For a college dropout, you mean?"

It wasn't what he'd meant at all, but she'd raised a question he'd been dying to know the answer to for years.

"Why'd you leave?" he asked gently. "Bonnie and I always

wondered."

A shadow flitted across her features. "Everything fell apart after my dad died, I guess. Or maybe it was just me." Her voice grew quiet. "I fell apart."

"Anyone would have. A loss like that..." He shook his head. "It's a lot to shoulder." After losing his mother when he was only thirteen, he understood that kind of pain first-hand.

"That's what your sister kept telling me." A sad smile tugged at her lips. "How is she, by the way? We lost touch after a while. My fault. Not hers."

"Married with a three-year-old kid. Living her best life." *Or so she claims.* Sometimes he wondered if things were as peachy as she pretended they were. The last time he'd visited her, there'd been something in her eyes when he'd asked about her husband. Something he couldn't quite define. All he knew was that the guy didn't seem to be around much.

"And practicing law by now, I presume?" Christie's expression was hungry for details.

He was more than happy to give them to her. "Nope. Instead of sitting for the bar exam, she eloped with one of her professors." Wes was pretty sure it was a decision she regretted, but it wasn't something they'd ever discussed.

"That sounds about right." A chuckle pealed out of Christie.

"Really?" Her answer surprised him. "I always felt like I was missing something when she showed up at our next family get-together, well...married." To a guy who was nearly a decade older than her, no less. It was ironic, considering how hard she'd ridden him over his crush on Christie.

Christie nodded, still chuckling. "Clearly, you weren't her college roommate."

"Clearly." He was dying for her to elaborate, but she didn't.

"So, where did Bonnie and her hottie professor end up?"

she probed merrily.

"They're still living in Stanford. He still teaches at the university."

"That's so...wow!" She made a soft humming sound. "I'm not even going to ask how they pulled that off without repercussions."

"Attorneys!" He figured that said it all.

She wrinkled her nose at him. "I wonder what she'd think of me reaching out to her after all this time."

He eagerly set his cell phone on the table and flipped it on. "I think it would mean the world to her. If you give me your number, I'll forward hers to you."

Her eyes widened on his phone. "I probably still have her number."

"You might not." He sobered as he nudged the phone closer to her. "She changed it after an ex-boyfriend gave her some trouble a few years back." Asking for advice from one of her professors about how to file a restraining order against him was how she'd landed on her husband's radar.

"Oh, I remember that." Christie sounded genuinely distressed. "You were out of town, and she couldn't reach you. She and I were both sort of freaking out about it."

"Yeah, I hate that I wasn't there." Wes had always suspected Dan had something to do with how quickly the situation had been resolved. However, it wasn't a conversation for a first date. "So, are you gonna give me your number or what?" He winked suggestively at her. "You never know when you might need a former detective on speed dial."

She chuckled again. "That wasn't nearly as subtle as your coin trick."

He held her gaze. "Maybe I wasn't going for subtle."

The color in her cheeks deepened as she recited her number for him. He added it to his contact list and immediately fired off a text to her.

I'm not part of the mix-up.

Her phone beeped with an incoming text. She pointed at the purse resting beside her on the seat. "Did you just...?"

"Yep."

Looking mystified, she dug her phone out of her purse and read his message. "What exactly are you trying to tell me?"

Before he could answer, Izzy arrived bearing their dinner plates on a tray. "Sorry that took so long, y'all. We're down a guy in the kitchen, so the two that are left are really hopping back there." She sounded a little out of breath as she set their plates in front of them. "What else can I get you?" She peeked over the top of Christie's mug. "Want a refill?"

"No, thank you." Christie fluttered a hand over the top of her mug. "I'm still working on this one."

Izzy frowned in concern as she lowered the tray to dangle against her side. "Do you like it?"

"Very much," Christie assured. "Enough to order it again."

"I'm glad to hear it." Izzy's shoulders relaxed. She flicked a questioning look at Wes. "Anything else I can get you, Wes?"

"I'm good. Thanks." He eyed his sandwich, which was already cut into halves. They were wrapped in brown parchment paper with the ends of the mixed grain bread sticking out, practically begging him to take a bite.

"Well, enjoy!" Izzy spun away and was soon bussing a table nearby.

Wes liked the fact that Christie didn't simply start eating. Instead, she shot him an expectant look, which told him she must be accustomed to saying grace first.

He stretched his arms across the table, palms facing up. He was pleased when she reached back without comment, resting her fingers lightly on top of his. They were sturdy hands that were accustomed to holding reins and pommels. Her nails were clipped short and painted solid white.

Someday he was going to ask about the tiny triangular shaped scar below the fingernail on her right forefinger.

Bowing his head, he said a quick prayer over their meal.

As she slid her hands away from his, he kept his fingers curled around hers to slow her retreat. The silky drag of her fingers across his made awareness zing between them.

He dove into the momentary pause in their conversation to explain his text. "The message I texted you was my way of saying I'm the guy you were supposed to meet for dinner this evening. I can't explain the mix up. I wasn't even aware Willa was trying to match you up with more than one guy." He wasn't too thrilled about it, either.

He picked up one of his sandwich halves and held it out to her.

She held up a hand, shaking her head. "I want to, but I can't."

"Just one bite, then," he coaxed, holding it closer to her. He knew she wanted it.

"Okay." Eyeing the sandwich wistfully, she guided his hand to her mouth and bit down. She leaned back and covered her mouth with her napkin while she chewed. "So good!" She chuckled after she swallowed. "I've never seen so many layers on a sandwich before."

She gestured at the sandwich half he was still holding. "Let me see it again."

Grinning, he pulled back more of the parchment paper to give her a better look.

She pointed out the layers, trying to identify each one. "That's squash puree on the bottom. Then sliced turkey." She frowned a little. "What's that chunky stuff on top of the turkey?"

He bent his head to peer more closely at it. "I think the menu said there was stuffing and a drizzle of gravy on the turkey."

"Are you serious?" She straightened in her seat. "It's like Thanksgiving all over again, except between two slices of bread."

"With cranberry sauce on top," he agreed, enjoying the fact that he'd talked her into taking a bite. "Want another bite?"

She made a face at him. "Want? Yes. Need? No."

Encouraged by her words, he held out the sandwich to her again. "It can be a small one if you want. This is too good not to share." *With my beautiful date.* He finished the sentence inside his head.

"Fine." She cupped his hand between hers as she took another bite, small enough that he wasn't sure she got all the layers this time. Regardless, he respected her wish to eat with moderation and didn't intend to keep pushing her. All he'd really wanted was the intimacy of sharing a sandwich with her.

It had been one of his biggest dreams in recent weeks to sit across the table from her like this.

And here we are.

"What are you thinking?" She crinkled her eyes at him. "It looks like the wheels in your head are spinning a mile per minute."

It was such an accurate assessment that he decided to humor her. "I didn't walk into this date blind like you did. I've been wanting to meet you, so I asked Willa to introduce us." He took another bite of his sandwich.

"Oh, wow!" Her eyes grew wide. "You actually knew it was me you were taking to dinner?"

"I did. Which is why I felt fully justified in coin flipping away the competition."

A soft, vulnerable light crept into her gaze. "You could've just come to one of my performances at Castellano's and met me that way."

"Really? Because I've tried." More times than he could count. He wrinkled his forehead at her. "You're not easy to track down afterward, Miss Hart."

She smiled shyly at him. "It's for security reasons. Though I'm still in the building, I make myself scarce immediately following the show."

"That's understandable." He liked the fact that she was continuing to watch her back, even after moving to such a small town.

"If you'd asked one of our staff members, though, they would've arranged for us to meet. They do it all the time."

"I like my methods better."

"A blind date, huh?" she mused.

"Only half blind," he corrected. "Like I said, I knew what I was getting into."

"Half knew," she clarified. "You didn't remember our first encounter until after the coin toss."

"How long are you going to hold that against me?" he teased, very much hoping she'd forgive him for that.

She narrowed her gaze playfully at him. "The jury's still out."

"It was a nice surprise to discover who you really are." Since they hadn't been doing much eating, he took advantage of the momentary lull in their conversation to polish off the first half of his sandwich. "Very nice," he added as he reached for the second half of his sandwich.

She poked her fork at her salad. "Are you still a mechanic?"

"I am. You've probably passed my new shop a thousand times." Her question was an abrupt reminder of how little she actually knew about him. He'd spent most of his career working as an undercover detective in Phoenix, so his mechanic shop there had merely been part of his cover. At least, that was how it had started out. Somewhere along the way, he'd discovered he was very good at tinkering beneath the hood of a car.

"Ah! You must be talking about Pinetop Auto." She looked intrigued. "How did you ever get such a normal sounding name through the local Chamber of Commerce? I would've expected them to make you change it to something more festive. Like..." She pursed her lips for a moment. "Red Nose Detailing. Or Stripes and Things. No, wait a sec!" He could tell she was warming to the topic. "How about the Sleigh Bay?" She waved a hand grandly through the air as she unveiled her latest brainstorm.

"I'm not sure what I did to earn such a roasting from you." She was laying it on pretty thick.

"What? You don't like my ideas?" She adopted an inno-cent look.

"I'm a simple guy, Christie." He snorted as he repeated her first suggestion. "Red Nose Detailing? Please tell me you're kidding!"

"I'm totally kidding!" She dissolved into laughter. "Your expression is priceless, though."

"Glad I could provide you with so much amusement." He settled back in his seat, thoroughly enjoying her smile and laughter. "Enough about my boring old auto body shop. I want to hear more about how a pre-law student ended up becoming a world-class trick rider."

"Like I said," her smile dimmed, "everything sort of fell apart when my dad died. He was the glue that held every-thing together in our little family. My mom was as lost as I was. After twenty-something years of being a housewife, she took up modeling."

"Modeling!" He cocked his head at her. "The kind that involves long runways and massive amounts of makeup?"

"And near starvation, yes." Her voice was dry. "She tried to get me to join her, but I refused. I picked my own adventure and buried my grief in horse therapy instead."

"I see." He was beginning to connect the dots. "And discovered you were something of a horse whisperer?" Kind of like he'd discovered he had a knack for fixing cars.

"Yes." Her smile returned. "In some ways, trick riding saved my life. I'm fortunate the Lord allowed me to cross paths with such an incredible trainer. Someone who believed in me and refused to give up on me, even while I was busy flunking out of college."

That last detail made Wes frown. "Bonnie never mentioned anything about you flunking your classes."

"She didn't know," Christie informed him flatly. "Very few people did. I, um...shut everyone else out. I'm not going to sit here and claim it was healthy, but it was my process for coping with my grief at the time." She idly twirled the lettuce with her fork. "It was just me, my horse, and hour after hour of training in the ring together. During the first few months, I about worked myself into the ground, but it was better than binge eating my way into an early grave. As the extra pounds started to melt off, I eventually got inspired to make other changes in my life, which was totally empowering." Her eyes glowed at the memory. "I suddenly realized I could achieve anything I wanted to if I worked hard enough for it."

"And you used that momentum to propel you up the charts," he concluded for her.

"Yes." She gave him a tremulous smile. "Grief changes you forever, Wes. Some people let it destroy them. As a woman of faith, I chose to channel it. To let it push me forward instead of pulling me backward. I know that may sound crazy—"

"It doesn't." He knew he was staring at her, but he couldn't help it. He was in complete awe of her. If she saw some hint of that in his expression, so be it. They were on a date, after all.

"Say something," she pleaded.

"I think you're amazing, Christie Hart."

"Really?" She fluttered her hands nervously in the air. "After everything I just told you? After all my setbacks and struggles..." She smiled helplessly at him.

He found it endearing that someone as successful as her was looking for reassurances from him. "Honestly, Christie? Everything you've told me this evening makes me admire you even more. Sure, I wanted to meet the beautiful, talented woman on the posters and billboards around town. Who wouldn't? But finding out who you really are...and what you're really made of despite all the challenges you faced along the way..." He shook his head, chuckling quietly to himself. "I want to date you," he confessed. There was no Bonnie Wakefield to warn him away this time. "I don't want tonight to be a one-time thing."

"Okay." She caught her lower lip between her teeth. "I... I'd like that, too."

The vulnerable side of her was so sweetly unexpected that it stirred him deeply. He longed to spend more time with her, exploring that sweetness.

An idea popped into his mind. "For our next date, would you like to go on one of those sleigh rides Pinetop is so famous for?" *Or buggy rides.* The owner, Flash Billings, alternated between his big red sleigh and ornate white buggy, depending on the weather and the state of the roads.

"Absolutely!" She nodded happily. "As long as it comes with coffee."

"Deal." He nodded at her mug. "An easier task now that I know what you like."

"You know a lot more about me than I intended to share. I can't believe how much I've unloaded on you tonight." She finally took a bite of her salad. It wasn't a big bite, more of a nibble.

"I don't mind. I've been told I'm a good listener." He'd mostly been told that by his long list of police informants, but still. He finished the second half of his sandwich, trying not to dwell on how lonely his choice of careers as a police detective had been. It was nice having someone sitting across the table from him to share things with like this. Really nice.

"You're an excellent listener," she assured warmly, "but we've talked way too much about me and not nearly enough about you." She took another bite of her salad.

He'd done it out of sheer habit. While working undercover, he'd grown skilled at talking up a storm without sharing anything of substance about himself. "There's not much to tell."

"I don't believe that for a second." She waved her fork in warning at him. "Everyone has a story, and I want to hear yours."

Her request warmed his heart. He was more than willing to share his story with her. Just not tonight. He wanted one evening with her thinking of him as a regular guy before she found out the truth.

He changed the subject by nodding at the salad she'd stopped eating. "Are you ready to box that up and take it with you?"

"Very ready." She flagged Izzy down and requested a to-go box and their check.

"Which I'll take," he interjected firmly. "Tonight is my treat." No way was he letting her pick up the tab on their first date.

"I'll go ring up your order." Izzy wagged a warning finger at him. "Just to be clear, winning the coin toss and paying for dinner this evening doesn't mean you've permanently edged Roman out of this." She twirled a hand through the air, including Christie in the gesture.

Christie waited until she walked away with his credit card

before dissolving into mirth. "Izzy has no idea just how hard you've been working to edge her brother out of the picture. I'm thinking it would be best to leave her in the dark."

"Agreed." He wasn't too bothered about it. "She'll figure it out soon enough."

Christie gave him another shy smile.

He hoped it meant she didn't object to his shameless intent to pursue her.

While they waited for Izzy to return, he took a long, sweeping look around the dining room. Like he did at every restaurant he patronized, he'd purposely claimed the side of the booth that faced the front entrance. Remaining vigilant was something that was deeply ingrained in him. Even after he finished tying up a few loose ends at the police depart-ment and left the force behind for good, he'd probably continue sleeping with one eye open.

Throughout dinner, he'd been mentally cataloguing the movements of everyone around them — the customer with bladder problems on his third trip to the restroom, the elderly woman who'd managed to sneak in a toy poodle via her oversized purse, and the young couple in the far corner of the room who'd been necking their way through dinner. Lucky them! He was hoping to steal a kiss from Christie at the end of the evening, but there were never any guarantees of that on a first date.

The only person in the vicinity who'd struck him as even remotely suspicious was a gaunt faced little fellow in faded overalls and suspenders. He was seated alone in the booth next to theirs. Though he was facing Wes, he'd spent the entire meal with a newspaper raised in front of his face. Every once in a while, he'd lower it long enough to take a slurp of his coffee. Then he'd returned to reading.

Wes did stuff like that when he was on official stakeouts, but nothing about the fellow behind the newspaper suggested he was a lawman. He had a severely discolored right canine tooth and bags beneath his eyes that suggested he'd not gotten much sleep lately.

Izzy glided in their direction, reclaiming his attention. She had his credit card and receipt in one hand and a pot of coffee in the other hand. She paused at the table of Mr. Tired in Overalls to top off his coffee on her way to their table. He offered her a simple thank you. Wes couldn't hear it from this far away, but he could read the guy's cracked lips.

Izzy finished making her way to their table and handed Wes his credit card and receipt. Then she produced a ballpoint pen and laid it on the table.

While she was making small talk with Christie, he signed the receipt and left her a generous tip.

"*Gracias!*" She beamed a grateful smile at him as she pocketed the pen and tucked the receipt into her little black book. "*Buenas noches.*"

"Goodnight, Izzy." He stood and held out a hand to Christie, assisting her out of her side of the booth. While she looped her crossbody purse over her head and reached for the handles of the bag holding her to-go box, he took the opportunity to dip his head closer to their waitress.

He spoke in undertones for her ears alone. "Please match your brother with someone else."

She pouted prettily up at him. "Are you sure about this, Wes?" Her voice was barely above a whisper.

"Very sure, Izzy." He silently begged her to understand. Roman was a good friend, and he didn't want to do anything to ruin that.

"Fine." Her lips flatlined. "But you've gotta help me get him out of the house more." The volume of her voice rose. Wes had no doubt that Christie could hear every word she said next. "Take him out for some bro time or something, alright?"

"I'll call him in the morning," he promised.

"*Gracias*," she repeated softly. "He's a good guy, Wes. He didn't deserve what happened."

"I know." He leaned closer to wrap her in a tender hug.

Her eyes were damp when he released her.

Christie touched his arm as they turned together to stroll past the table of Mr. Tired in Overalls. "What was that about?"

He glanced down at her hand on his arm, liking the way it looked there. "She's worried about her brother. Wants me to look in on him more."

"I heard that part." She playfully squeezed his arm. "I was referring to all the whispering the two of you were doing behind my back."

"You don't miss much, do you?" They were standing close enough for him to catch a whiff of her flowery shampoo. Only because his face was turned toward her did he notice the reaction of the man in overalls as they passed by his booth.

As his tired gaze landed on Christie, hunger shuddered through him. It made Wes think of a ravenous wolf licking his chops.

He bustled her out of the bistro as quickly as he could.

She was frowning worriedly by the time they reached the sidewalk. "Is everything okay?"

He glanced back at the glass door swinging closed behind them. "Yeah." *I hope so.* "Just didn't like the way that guy was looking at you."

"What guy?" She shivered and stepped closer to him, something he didn't mind one bit.

"The one in overalls in the booth next to ours." He slung a protective arm around her as they continued their promenade down the sidewalk. She leaned against his side, making a scoffing sound. "Not to sound full of myself, but lots of people stare at me in public. That's what happens when your face ends up on as many posters as mine does."

She wasn't joking, either. Castellano's had been heavily advertising her presence in Pinetop ever since her arrival in June. She was their biggest headline, helping them draw crowds from every town within driving distance. He had no doubt she was the reason their new indoor rodeo production had been such a success.

He hugged her tighter. "I'd like to walk you to your car, if that's okay."

"I'd appreciate that." She shivered and burrowed closer to him.

He could've kicked himself for forgetting how cold she'd been outside earlier. As he reached for the zipper of his jacket, she stopped him with her words.

"Don't. It's a short walk to where I'm parked." She pointed. "I'm in the white Jeep against the curb."

He followed her gloved finger and discovered she was referring to a Jeep Grand Cherokee. "Nice wheels." At a quick glance, though, there were several updates he'd gladly make to it.

"I'm glad you approve, car man."

"I do." She'd sprung for the upgraded Summit Reserve model, which had set her back about seventy grand. However, it still only had the standard wheels package. He mentally replaced them with extra wide tires, matte black hubcaps, and added a few strips of aqua blue undercarriage lighting.

They paused beside the door on the driver's side.

He pivoted to face her, longing to kiss her goodnight. His gaze settled on her mouth. She'd applied a layer of lip gloss before leaving the bistro.

She gave a soft, breathy chuckle, glancing around them and making her breath glow whitely in the frosty air. "The

Christmas lights have Main Street lit up like the Fourth of July, don't they?"

"Yeah." He imagined what it would feel like the first time his mouth touched hers. Her lips would be much warmer than the frigid mountain temperatures.

As if feeling his perusal, her fingers tightened on the to-go bag in her hand. "What are we doing, Wes?" she whispered, tipping her face up to his.

"Dating, I hope." It felt like this moment had been a long time coming for them. Years in the making. Finding her, losing her, and finding her again. She'd been worth the wait, though.

"It feels a little crazy, doesn't it?" She anxiously scanned his features. "You and me? After all this time?"

If by crazy, she meant perfect, then he agreed wholeheartedly. Her nervousness, however, was palpable, making him decide there was no need to rush their first kiss.

"I'll call you," he promised, reaching out to brush his thumb against her chin.

She caught her breath, parting her lips so temptingly that he nearly changed his mind about going slow with her.

It took an enormous act of willpower to drop his hand.

While she fumbled with her remote to unlock the car, he reached around her to open the door for her.

"Thanks, Wes." She sounded a little out of breath. "For everything. Tonight was...special." She hurriedly slid behind the wheel.

"Yeah. For me, too." He allowed his gaze to trace the curve of her cheek and the perfect bow of her lips as he shut the door for her.

It was a date that almost hadn't happened with a girl he thought he'd never see again. And now he was counting the minutes until their second date.

CHAPTER 3: MAMA DRAMA

CHRISTIE

C hristie's alarm went off way too early the next morning.

"Just stop already!" She reached blindly for the nightstand, groping for her cell phone that was plugged into its charger.

Despite her frantic tapping against the screen, it continued to ring. On the fifth or sixth ring, it dawned on her that it wasn't her alarm clock sounding off, after all. She was receiving a phone call.

With a groan of protest, she sat up in bed and switched on her Tiffany lamp. The glass dragonfly dome cast a prism of light against the walls and ceiling.

Her phone continued to ring shrilly, giving her the start of a headache.

Snatching it up, she glanced at the caller ID before accepting the call. "Oh, my goodness! Mom? Is everything okay?" She rubbed her eyes, wondering why her mother was calling her in the middle of the night.

"Yes. Why wouldn't it be?"

"Uh...maybe because it's three in the morning." Christie silently begged her mother to hurry up and say what was on her mind so they could both get back to bed.

"I miss you, baby."

Whatever. No matter how tired Christie was, she wasn't falling for that line. Ruby Hart only called when she had an agenda in mind, and it was always self-serving and layered with criticism. The woman was literally impossible to please.

"Aren't you going to say anything back?" she demanded petulantly.

"I miss you, too, Mom," Christie lied, trying to smother a yawn. Though she didn't succeed, she managed to keep it silent.

"It's not worth as much if I have to drag the words out of you."

Here we go. "Plus, I love you." That part was true, at least. No matter how mad her mother made her, Christie was a big believer in the kill-her-with-kindness theory. Sometimes it worked, and sometimes it didn't. It depended on what kind of mood she happened to be in.

"Better," Ruby Hart conceded in a grudging voice.

Christie tangled her fingers in the velvet plush gray blanket covering her bed and plopped back against the lilac pillow shams, waiting.

And waited some more.

And waited some more.

Her mother would eventually get around to telling her why she'd called.

"Okay. You win." Ruby Hart finally let out a long, gusty sigh. "I need your help with something."

"Sure." Christie's hand tightened on the phone. "Anything."

"Really? You haven't even heard my request yet."

"You're my mother," Christie reminded softly. "Whatever

you need, just tell me." She had plenty of money these days. Her mother knew that.

"Fine. I need a place to stay. Just for a few weeks."

Christie frowned at the ceiling. "Why's that?" Her mother lived in a luxury condo. She additionally owned a beach home in Florida. Come to think of it, Florida was where she normally spent the winter months — sipping peach tea and playing dominoes and cards with her snow bird friends.

"I just broke up with my boyfriend, and he wasn't too happy about it." Her mother's voice grew brittle. "They always get so attached," she complained. "You go out for a few nice dinners and have a nice time. But once you reach the kissing stage, they start making noises about long-term commitments. It's downhill from there."

If you say so. Christie didn't have much dating experience to tap into, so she had precious few nuggets of wisdom to offer on the topic. Her blind date with Wes yesterday evening was the first date she'd been on in...*sheesh!* Two years, maybe? However, her mother seemed to be waiting for an answer, so she scrambled to give her one.

"I, um...I'm sorry to hear about your breakup." It was a lame answer, but it was all she could come up with on the fly. "And you can totally come visit me anytime." She grimaced as she glanced around her second-story bedroom in the little mountain chalet she'd purchased last summer.

Though it had two bedrooms and two bathrooms, the master bedroom was the only one she'd bothered furnishing. She wondered when her mother planned on making her appearance and whether it would leave her with enough time to hit up a furniture store.

"How does later today sound?" Ruby Hart inquired quickly. "I could catch a flight to Phoenix and rent a car to drive the rest of the way."

Today? Wow! Okay. Christie started a mental list of all the things she'd have to do between now and then, like purchase an air mattress for the spare bedroom. For herself, of course. So much for going furniture shopping between now and then! There'd be no time for that. She'd just offer her mother the master bedroom and be done with it.

"Please rent an SUV, and make sure it has snow tires," she advised. "There's snow in the forecast." Even if her mother caught an early flight out of Dallas, she probably wouldn't arrive until dinner time. The drive up from Phoenix was going to take between three and four hours, depending on traffic.

In the meantime, Christie would get one of the shops on Main Street to prepare a charcuterie tray to have waiting in the fridge — something as pretty as it was scrumptious. She hoped it would bring a smile to her mother's face, since she was a bit of a food snob.

"Snow? Ugh!" Ruby Hart made a sound of distaste. "How can you stand living up in the mountains where it's so cold?"

"You get used to it, I guess." Christie honestly wasn't sure she'd ever get used to the mountain winds or the mounds of snow they blew in. However, Wes's borrowed jacket had provided an excellent buffer last night against their bite. And the way his eyes had kissed her at the end of the evening had warmed her to the point of nearly melting. She sighed at the memory.

"Are you sick?" her mother demanded. "You sound like you're getting sick."

"No. Just a little tired, but that's okay," she added before her mom could lapse into one of her nauseating speeches about good sleep hygiene. "Tomorrow is Saturday, so I can sleep in."

"I hope that means I'm not interrupting anything." Her mother's voice turned sly. "I know you're all grown up now and have a life of your own."

"Nope. You're not interrupting anything." Christie rolled her eyes, well aware of where their conversation was heading.

"If there's someone special in your life, I certainly don't want to be a third wheel."

"There's not." Christie kept her voice carefully bland. Though she felt a little guilty about not telling the whole truth, she didn't think a single blind date with Wes Wakefield counted as being in a relationship. Not yet, anyway.

"You mean you're not dating *anyone?*" Her mother's voice rose to an incredulous note.

"I date a little." She was way too tired to go into the details right now.

"Define *a little*."

At three in the morning? Christie gave a silent sigh. "I went on a blind date last night."

"And?"

"He was nice."

"You are so full of details." Her mother's voice was sarcastic. "Did you kiss?"

There was no way Christie was touching that one. "He invited me on a sleigh ride. We haven't hammered down a time yet."

"Sounds to me like it was a successful evening, since it's leading to a second date." Her mother's voice was infused with curiosity. "What's his name?"

"Wes."

"What does he do for a living?"

It was all Christie could do to hold back a laugh, knowing her mother wasn't going to like her answer. "He's a mechanic."

"A what?" Ruby Hart's voice rose to just shy of a shriek.

"Relax. He owns his own shop, Mom." Christie grinned into the darkness, enjoying her mother's reaction a little too much.

"I don't care if he manufactures his own auto parts out of pure gold, darling!"

Here it comes.

"You're Christie Hart! A champion rodeo rider."

You can do so much better than him. Blah, blah, blah... Christie had heard the speech too many times to count. She tuned her mother out, eyeing the textured paint on the trayed ceiling, while idly wondering if she should change the pale blue-green accent layer up there to a European white that matched the walls. It glowed a pearlized shade of gray in the moonlight pouring through her balcony windows.

"Are you even listening to me, Christie Rosalie Hart?" her mother demanded after a while.

"Yes." She could repeat the entire speech by heart if she had to. She'd heard it dozens of times.

"Well, do you have anything to say for yourself?"

Nothing you want to hear. After a moment of deliberation, she decided to take the high road. "Go easy on me, Mom. I'm married to my career, which means I don't get out much." She blinked a few times to sever the distant stare she'd been giving the ceiling. "Moving to Pinetop was my way of slowing the pace a little. Baby steps, right?"

"Would it have killed you to pick a town with a bigger dating pool?"

"I'd rather answer that question after you see Pinetop for yourself." Though Christie wasn't holding her breath, it was possible that the Christmas charm of the remote mountain town might soften her mother's heart a little.

"I can't imagine there being much to see in a town that small," Ruby Hart grumbled.

"There's me," Christie reminded brightly. When her mother didn't answer, she added, "I'm looking forward to seeing you." It was only a partial fib. She usually enjoyed the first five minutes of their visits. After that, things tended to get a little dicey.

"Me, too. We'll talk more in the morning. Love you."

"Love you, too, Mom." She waited for her mother to disconnect the line so she couldn't be accused of hanging up on her, another hard lesson she'd learned over the years.

Sleep evaded her for the rest of the night, making her really glad it was Saturday. She stumbled down the stairs and entered her tiny kitchen at the crack of eight to turn on her coffee dispenser. The only way she was going to push through her tiredness today was if she was properly caffeinated.

As she was lifting her first cup of coffee to her mouth, her cell phone rang. The thought crossed her mind that it shouldn't be legal for moms to call their daughters before their first cup of coffee.

Regardless, she lifted the phone to her ear. "Hello?"

"Morning, Christie." It was Wes.

"Oh, hey!" Though her brain was moving in slow motion like the rest of her, she was really glad to hear his voice instead of her mother's.

"You sound tired. Did I wake you?" He sounded regretful.

"What you're hearing is relief," she assured him with a yawn.

"Oh?"

"Over the fact that you're not somebody else."

He snorted out a laugh. "I feel like I'm missing part of the story."

"My mother called in the middle of the night." She muffled another yawn, unsure if she was making much sense. "She's, um...difficult."

"I'm sorry to hear it." His voice was so cautious that she smiled.

"By difficult," she clarified with a chuckle, "we're talking about a woman who could star in an adult version of Mean Girls. And if there was an Olympic medal for how many criticisms a person could stuff into a single sentence—"

Wes burst out laughing. "Man, Christie! You're hilarious when you're tired."

"And stressed," she pointed out. "It's a lethal combination. My mother is the one person in the world who can drive me to binge eat donuts."

"That's it. I'm coming over to comfort you."

She could hear a rustling sound in the background.

"How do you know where I live?"

"I ran a background check on you."

"You what?" She wasn't sure she'd heard right.

"Just kidding. Willa told me where you live. The background check was a policeman joke."

She was more confused than ever. "Why are you regaling me with cop humor all of a sudden?"

"It would make more sense if I explain that in person."

Her hand flew to her sleep-tousled hair. "You really, really, really don't want to see me like this," she warned in a strained voice.

"Why? Are you dressed?"

"Only if gray yoga pants and oversized sweatshirts count as dressed." It was the same outfit she'd slept in.

"They count."

"I have bed head, no makeup on, and I'm not even halfway through my first cup of coffee."

"If we're going to date, I'm bound to see you with messy hair at some point."

"Not the morning after our first date, though," she squeaked.

"You're the most beautiful woman I've ever met. I'm sure I can handle the no makeup version of you."

Though she knew he was only being nice, his words made her heart beat a little faster. "Don't say I didn't warn you."

"I won't."

The warmth in his voice was more soothing than the second cup of coffee she'd be holding shortly. She shoved another cup beneath the dispenser and hit the start button. "If I can find my brush, I'll at least straighten my hair before you get here."

He chuckled. "I'll see you in a few minutes."

She shuffled back up the stairs and bumped her hip on the doorway as she re-entered her bedroom. "Ow!" She rubbed the sore spot, nearly spilling the coffee she was still clutching like a lifeline.

In the end, she managed to locate her brush and twist her hair into some semblance of a ponytail. It was crooked, but she'd already warned Wes to lower his expectations.

She debated whether to change her pale pink sweatshirt but decided she was too tired to coordinate a better outfit. What she was wearing was clean, and nobody was expecting her to be dressed up on a Saturday morning, certainly not Wes. He was the most easygoing guy she'd ever met. He was also fun to be around, admiring, and downright appreciative of the time they'd gotten to spend together last night.

Before she left the bathroom, she brushed her teeth a second time. She'd already brushed them when she'd first rolled out of bed, but it seemed like a wise thing to do since her sort-of-almost-maybe-potential-future boyfriend was on his way to see her.

No sooner had she exited her bedroom did a knock sound on the front door. She slid a hand along the stairwell railing for support as she made her way down the stairs. Sometimes when she was this tired, her equilibrium was thrown off a little.

She reached the front door, pulled back the latch on the deadbolt, and swung it open. "Hey, Wes!" She gestured for him to step inside.

Fortunately, he moved quickly, because a blistering wind was blowing outside.

She was shivering by the time she closed the door behind him.

They faced each other, smiling, in the entry foyer. He'd ditched the black jeans he'd been wearing last night in favor of blue jeans and a plaid shirt. The tails of it were hanging out beneath his brown suede jacket. He was still in his Stetson and boots. What put her the most at ease, though, was the fact that he hadn't shaved. Dark stubble covered the hard lines of his squared off jaw.

"You look amazing," he informed her quietly, drinking her in with his gaze the same way she was drinking him in. "I knew you would, with or without makeup."

"Only because I found my brush." She chuckled, reaching for the end of her ponytail and tossing it playfully over her shoulder. Unfortunately, the movement threw her off balance.

"Whoa!" He reached out to remove her cup of coffee and set it on the marble-topped cabinet in the foyer.

She ended up in the loose circle of his arms. "Wes..." Her hands curled around the lapels of his jacket.

"I'm right here, Christie." His warm brown gaze grew hooded as he gazed down at her.

"I'm really..." She swayed closer, initially intending to tell him how tired she was.

She didn't get the first word out before he dipped his head and caught her mouth in a tender kiss.

It was so wonderful that she burrowed closer, soaking in his warmth, strength, and good, clean scent. "Wes," she whispered again when he raised his head.

"Yeah?"

"That was unexpected." She couldn't believe the man of her dreams had actually kissed her.

"I'm sorry if it was too soon."

"No, we're good. I liked it." That was putting it mildly. His kiss had far exceeded her many daydreams.

"Me, too." He seemed in no hurry to drop his arms from around her. "I know we've only been on one date so far, but will you be my girl?"

She grew still for a moment. "I, um...yes." A nervous chuckle escaped her. Was he for real?

"You don't sound too sure about that answer." His dark gaze scraped across her features. "If I'm moving too fast, just say so."

"Not at all. I was just trying to figure out if this was really happening, as opposed to dreaming up your entire visit. I'm that tired," she confessed, muffling another yawn with a hand over her mouth.

He smiled, looking relieved. "I assure you this is really happening." He abruptly bent to hook an arm beneath her legs.

"What are you—Wes!" she squealed as she tumbled, laughing, against his chest. She twined her arms around his neck and held on while he carried her to the sofa in the living room. It had overstuffed gray cushions in a soft suede fabric.

He gently laid her on it, tucking one of her throw pillows beneath her head.

"Thanks." Her eyelids started to droop. "If you don't mind locking the door before letting yourself out..." She wasn't sure she had the energy to get back up and throw the deadbolt in place.

"I don't mind at all." She felt his lips brush her forehead. "I'll call you later. Get some rest."

"I will." She blindly reached for him.

He caught her hand and gave it a gentle squeeze.

"You never told me why you were cracking cop jokes earlier," she reminded in a sleepy voice.

She thought he said, "Because I'm a policeman," but she might have dreamed it since she was already drifting.

He spread a quilt over her and tucked it around her chin. It was the last thing she remembered.

HER PHONE JANGLED WITH AN INCOMING CALL, YANKING her out of her slumber. She sat up, stretching her arms high over her head and wondering how long she'd been asleep.

She blushed as the memory of Wes carrying her to the couch came flooding back. She'd been deliriously tired during his visit, laughing at the silliest things and talking out of her head. He probably thought she was a complete nut job.

Well, maybe not a complete one, since he'd asked her out on a second date. And asked her to be his girlfriend.

I have a boyfriend. A surreal feeling washed over her as the phone stopped ringing. After being alone for so long, she suddenly, well, wasn't alone. Their relationship was moving kind of fast, but she chalked that up to them previously knowing each other. That, and the fact that she'd been wildly attracted to him for a long, long, long time...as in nine of her twenty-seven years.

Her phone started ringing again from somewhere in the house.

With a sigh of resignation, she pushed away the quilt, threw her bare feet over the side of the sofa, and stood. She followed the ringing sound toward the kitchen. Her cozy mountain home boasted an open floor plan, so the only thing separating the kitchen from the living room was a granite topped bar and a trio of stools.

It was a newly renovated chalet on the main road heading down the mountain. Unlike most of the other homes in town, it wasn't part of any subdivision. Instead, it was tucked away in a copse of evergreens, roughly halfway between downtown and the nearest subdivision. According to her real estate agent, it had belonged to the head forest ranger in Pinetop, a man who had since gotten married and relocated to a larger home.

She was a little surprised he hadn't put an addition on the chalet and stayed put. There was plenty of room to add on since it had been built on an oversized lot. According to the survey, her home was sitting on nearly a full acre. And because of its location on the side of the mountain, she had an incredible view.

As she sought out her ringing phone, a prayer bubbled to her lips.

Please let me stay here, Lord.

After years of being on the road, she was ready to put down roots. Though she'd only been in Pinetop for six months, her cozy little chalet already felt like home. It was quiet and peaceful, a place to rest both body and soul.

She finally located her phone. It was laying beside the coffee dispenser, half covered by a dish towel. It stopped ringing the moment she picked it up. Her heart sank at the realization she'd missed umpteen calls from her mother.

Uh-oh.

She scanned the digital time displayed on the face of her phone in disbelief. It was later than she'd been expecting — much later — at half-past six. She'd slept all the way until dinnertime.

How was that even possible? She'd only meant to take a nap. She glanced frantically around her, knowing her all-day snooze fest meant she hadn't done the first thing to prepare for her mother's arrival. There were dirty coffee mugs in the sink, linens to change in the master bedroom, and an air mattress still to purchase for the spare room.

Unless I sleep on the couch tonight.

She eyed the rumpled quilt lying across the cushions. Calling it comfortable would be an understatement. She'd been crashed out on its plush cushions for nearly nine hours.

A knock sounded on the front door.

She froze, feeling like a cornered chicken with a pack of wolves closing in on her. She needed more time to make the house presentable before her mother arrived. A few minutes, at least.

"Christie," a woman called shrilly. "Are you in there?"

Too late! Christie grew still at the sound of her mother's voice, realizing her wish for a little more time wasn't going to be granted.

"Coming!" Dragging her feet across the living room, she reluctantly pulled open the door.

"It took you long enough!" Her mother stood on the front porch, shivering in some over-the-top black bodysuit that looked sprayed on. A brown grocery bag was clutched in one arm. She was waving her cell phone irritably in the other. "I've been calling and calling and calling!"

"Hi, Mom!" It was so cold outside that Christie reached out to tug her mother across the threshold, kicking the door shut behind her.

"Hi, hon!" Ruby Hart gave her a brief, one-armed hug before pulling back. "Why didn't you answer your phone?" A wrinkle scrunched the middle of her otherwise smooth forehead. Like every other part of her face, it had been nipped, tucked, or plumped out with various cosmetic procedures.

Christie spread her hands and debated her options. She

ultimately decided to spring for the truth. Or part of it, anyway. "It's Saturday, so I slept in."

"You slept all day?" Her mother's gasp of censure filled the room. "That's downright unhealthy. It'll throw off your sleep cycle and—"

"You're right. It was a huge mistake," Christie interrupted, not wanting to hear another lecture she already had memorized. Her mother had been warning her about the horrors of sleep deprivation since her sleep-walking episode at the age of five. As far as she knew, it had been a onetime thing.

Ruby Hart nodded to acknowledge the white flag her daughter had raised. Her platinum blonde hair was piled high on her head, anchored against the wind with countless hairpins. Her feet were encased in ankle boots with wedge heels that couldn't have been easy to walk up the icy porch stairs in. However, Christie didn't dare comment on them. At the age of forty-nine, her mother had solidly arrived at middle age, but she was fighting it every step of the way.

"I have something really unfortunate to tell you," she announced as she plopped her grocery bag on the granite countertop. Her icy blue gaze glittered with more excitement than distress. She didn't simply suffer from a tinge of paranoia. She reveled and wallowed in it. She especially loved being the bearer of bad news.

"Uh-oh! Lay it on me, Mom." Christie motioned for her to continue, fully expecting a Santa-sized list of complaints about the dusty grocery store shelves or lack of available products in the too-small town she'd chosen to move to.

"As you can see, I stopped off at the grocery store on my way here," her mother disclosed in a mildly scolding voice. "I know how little time you spend at home, so I figured your pantry and fridge were empty."

Christie didn't answer, knowing it wouldn't have mattered if her cupboards were fully stocked. Her mother was usually on some trendy diet, and each one came with a long list of special dietary needs that were impossible to anticipate before her arrival. Sometimes it was no meat. Sometimes it was no carbs. Sometimes it was no sugar. On one of her visits, she'd even been experimenting with intermittent fasting. Christie didn't understand the intermittent part, since she hadn't seen her mother take a single bite of food during her entire visit.

Her mother abruptly spun around to face her, slapping her hands down on her desperately thin hips. She'd lost weight again. She was so skinny now that she was at real risk of being blown away by the fierce mountain wind outside.

"I asked around about your new boyfriend while I was in town."

"What are you talking about?" Christie wasn't sure how her mother had found out about Wes's status as her boyfriend, since it had happened *after* their middle-of-the-night telephone conversation.

"I know, I know." Her mother waved away her protest. "It's not official, since you've only been on one date, but he *will* ask you out. They always do. It's the curse of the Hart women."

Christie's breath eased out at the realization that her mother wasn't, in fact, in possession of her newest, most precious secret. She was just being her usual dramatic self.

"And before you flip out about it," her mother continued, "I assure you I was discreet with my questions. I merely pretended like I needed some work done on my car."

"On your rental car?" Christie's eyebrows flew upward. "I thought I told you an SUV would be better for these roads!"

"You did. Relax, hon. I rented a Tahoe." Her mother waved a hand irritably and returned to her story. "Bottom line is this. Wes Wakefield isn't who he says he is."

Christie stared at her in disbelief. Though her mother had

made it perfectly clear over the phone that she didn't approve of Wes's choice of vocation, this was taking things a little too far, even for her.

"He's a cop," her mother continued in a rush. "Or was before he became a mechanic. That's an odd transition, don't you think? He clearly has something to hide." She shook her head, looking displeased. "Anyhow, he followed some woman named Tess into town. It sounded like they might've been closer than friends at some point. He served as her bodyguard of sorts before she got married."

Christie blinked rapidly, hardly knowing how to respond to such a flood of information.

"Not to him," her mother hastened to add. "He's still single, but he might still have feelings for her, which would make him a home wrecker if—"

"Mom!" Christie halted her mother's tirade with an upraised hand. "Just...stop. Please."

"If you insist." Her mother sounded taken aback. "I'm only trying to look out for you. The world is full of crazies. You don't need to treat me like I'm..." She shook her head, searching for the right word.

One of the crazies you're always in such a tizzy about? Christie mentally supplied her own explanation for her mother's endless list of issues. Not for the first time, she wondered how they could be related. Though they bore a physical resemblance, they had nothing in common. Literally nothing.

Her mother was a pencil-thin shopaholic, social butterfly, and health nut. In contrast, Christie was a curvy introvert and foodie who preferred the company of horses over people. They were polar opposites in, well, everything.

"I just want what's best for you, darling," her mother announced with a triumphant smile, probably thinking she'd latched onto something her daughter couldn't argue with. "And if Wes isn't what's best for you—"

"I know he's a cop," Christie retorted in a tight voice. "Or was," she clarified. "He told me." *And then I fell asleep before he could explain himself.*

"He did?" Her mother's eyes widened a little. "Then why did you say he's a mechanic?"

"Because that's what he is now." Obviously, she and her new boyfriend had some more communicating to do. Maybe it wasn't too late to drive downtown to see about purchasing that air mattress, after all. Maybe she'd drive past Pinetop Auto on her way to the store and see if Wes was there. His shop would be closed by now, but he'd made some comment about liking to get stuff done after hours. If he was still there, they could hopefully have that talk he'd been wanting to have with her earlier.

"Oh." Looking utterly deflated, her mother started pulling boxes and cans out of her grocery bag. Her movements were short and jerky, which meant she was either embarrassed or angry. Neither emotion ever looked good on her.

"I have to go." Christie spun away from her and headed for the stairs.

"Where?" Her mother glanced up in surprise as she jogged up the stairs.

"To meet with someone," she answered vaguely. "I won't be gone long." Her hands were shaking with a mixture of irritation and anger by the time she reached her bedroom. She yanked off the bed linens and swapped them out with clean ones from her lower dresser drawer. Then she pulled her lilac comforter over them. Folding her fluffy duvet, she laid it carefully across the foot of the bed.

She moved to her closet to stuff the dirty sheets in the tall laundry basket she kept there. After a moment of deliberation, she reached for her suitcase in the corner and started stuffing clothes and other necessities into it. On her way out, she snatched up her work boots and Stetson. Dragging all of it down the short hallway, she deposited the entire shebang in the middle of her empty spare room.

If things got bad enough between her and her mother, she was packed well enough to claim a last-minute work obligation and relocate to a hotel. She hoped it didn't come to that, but it wouldn't hurt to keep her options open. Ruby Hart had a way of driving her completely batty sometimes.

Returning to the master bedroom, she rummaged through her top dresser drawer to retrieve her keys and her father's old signet ring. He'd given it to her on his deathbed with an incoherent mumble she hadn't understood a word of. Her mother had turned the house inside out looking for it after he'd passed, but Christie had allowed her to continue thinking he'd lost it during his final hours on this earth.

Since it was the last thing her father had given her, it was very precious to her, something she had no intention of giving up to the woman who'd inherited the rest of Jimmy Hart's estate. Though it was something she and her mother never talked about, Christie's failing grades weren't the only reason she'd quit college. The other reason was because the funding for her tuition had stopped the day her father had died.

It was probably an oversight on her mother's part. In the end, it hadn't mattered since Christie had ultimately chosen to drop out of school. Regardless, her father's signet ring was hers and hers alone. Retrieving one of her winter jackets from her closet, she tucked it inside the fleece-lined pocket on the right. Then she stepped into a pair of snow boots and headed downstairs.

Her mother watched in disapproval as she stopped by the sofa on her march across the living room to fold the quilt she'd been cuddled beneath earlier.

"Have you been sleeping on the couch? What's wrong with your room?" Her mother glanced toward the stairs.

"Nothing is wrong with my room, Mom. I was just

napping in the living room. People do that." She grabbed her purse from her built-in desk in the corner of the kitchen, then reached for the handle of the door leading to the garage.

Ruby Hart followed her, fluttering her hands in agitation as she hurried down the steps to her lower-level garage. "I just got here. Are you sure your appointment isn't something that can be rescheduled?"

"It's not." That part of her story wasn't a complete lie, since Christie didn't have an official appointment with anyone.

"You know I don't like being alone." Her mother gave a nervous titter. "I bet that's not something you'd expect to hear from a grown woman, but it's true."

"This won't take long, Mom. An hour max. I promise." Christie was accustomed to soothing her mother's many fears. On top of her fear of being alone, she also didn't like the dark, elevators, airplanes, thunderstorms, or spiders. The list went on and on.

"Okay. I'm holding you to that." Her mother fluttered a hand in goodbye. "See you in an hour." Shivering, she shut the door.

Christie felt like she was escaping from jail as she took a seat behind the wheel of her Jeep Grand Cherokee. She mashed the button on her visor to open the garage door. Then she started her vehicle.

Or tried to.

It coughed to life, then immediately died. She tried to start the Jeep again with the same results. Something was wrong. Either the battery was dead, or the starter was defunct.

She sat back in her seat, feeling defeated. The Jeep had run just fine last night. It was only six months old. She'd purchased it upon her arrival in Pinetop. This shouldn't be happening.

She gripped the steering wheel with both hands. *So much for getting a break from my mother's miserable company. What to do...*

There was only one logical solution. The more Christie thought about it, the more she liked the idea. She reached for her phone and dialed the owner of Pinetop Auto.

Wes picked up right away. "Hey, you!" He sounded so glad to hear from her that it was difficult to put much stock in her mother's warnings about him and his biggest reason for moving to Pinetop — some woman named Tess.

She swallowed her misgivings. "Hey, Wes. I, um...have some not-so-good news." She cringed at her choice of words. They made her sound way too much like her mother.

"Okay." His voice grew cautious. "What's up?"

"My Jeep won't start," she sighed.

"I'll be right over," he said quickly. Maybe a little too quickly?

As soon as the thought crossed her mind, Christie felt guilty for thinking it. *Don't do this.* She closed her eyes and gave herself a mental shake, knowing she'd allowed her mother to get under her skin again. If she wasn't careful, the woman would have her jumping at shadows and second-guessing her own name.

Ruby Hart wasn't a normal mother. She was all too skilled at eroding her only daughter's confidence in everyone and everything around her. In the past, Christie had allowed her to separate her from friends and part-time jobs, even from stores she frequently shopped at.

Not this time.

She drew a deep, bracing breath. She'd finally struck out on her own seven years ago. Though her life had been full of normal ups and downs since then, she'd found no reason to constantly be looking over her shoulder the way her mother seemed to think everyone should.

I'm not living in fear of my own shadow like you do, Mom. Life was too short for that nonsense. *And I'm dating Wes Wakefield whether you like it or not.*

Another woman might've been his reason for coming into town, but Christie intended to be the reason he stayed.

CHAPTER 4: STALLED OUT

WES

Wes stuffed his cell phone in the back pocket of his jeans and stepped away from the pickup he'd been standing underneath. It was suspended in the air inside the auto bay on the far right of his shop. One of his new part-time mechanics, Felipe, was working on a car in the middle bay. He'd agreed to stay after hours this evening for some overtime pay to help wrap up a few projects.

Wes strode his way and waited until Felipe lifted his head from the hood before he started speaking.

Felipe wiped his greasy hands on his jeans as he glanced over at the truck Wes had been working on. "That was quick." He was a young and wiry seasonal worker from Christmas Tree Farm at the edge of town. Though he didn't possess any professional certifications, he'd agreed to some on-the-job training from Wes during the off season. He'd proven to be a quick learner.

"Oh, I'm not finished with the truck yet. I wish." Wes angled his head at the tow truck parked in the far left bay.

"Just got a call from someone whose car won't start. I may have to tow it in."

Felipe nodded, giving the shop a sweeping glance. "I should be done with this one in fifteen to twenty minutes. That'll free up a spot." He knew Wes preferred not to leave the tow truck parked outside during bad weather, and it looked like a storm might be blowing in.

"That would be great." Wes hopped into the truck and rolled down the window to lean out a few inches. "Listen, I really appreciate the extra hours you've been putting in lately." Felipe had been doing such a great job handling the routine stuff that Wes was toying with the idea of offering him something more permanent. He preferred to handle the more specialized jobs — detailing and custom upgrades. He had no idea if Felipe would give his offer any serious consideration, but it was worth a try.

"No problem, bro." Felipe shrugged, grinning. "Gotta have money for Christmas presents." He had a baseball cap on backwards and no wedding ring.

Wes pointed toward the back of the shop. "Don't forget about the donuts in the break room." A satisfied customer had dropped them off earlier. "Take 'em with you when you go." He knew there were a lot of mouths to feed at Christmas Tree Farm, many of them poor immigrants. They were a tight-knit bunch. Like family. It was something Wes had always envied about them.

"Thanks, man. The kids'll think Christmas came early." Felipe gave him a two-fingered salute and ducked back beneath the hood of the car he was working on. It was a simple oil change and general servicing that would require checking the filters and tire treads, as well as topping off the fluids.

Wes mashed a button on his remote. The tall garage door in front of him rolled open. As soon as the spring thaw hit, he planned to have a new steel garage installed on the concrete pad out back. It would free up the three auto bays in the front for routine repairs and maintenance, allowing him to handle all the custom detail work inside the new space.

His drive to Christie's chalet took less than five minutes. She lived in an area that the locals referred to as mid-town due to the cluster of subdivisions located there. A few miles beyond them was Christmas Tree Farm. Her home was the only one that wasn't part of any actual neighborhood. It was tucked away all by itself in a copse of evergreens, lending it a sense of privacy that was virtually unheard of in the otherwise crowded little tourist town.

He pulled into her long paved driveway and followed it around the curve to her home. The rustic little chalet was perched on the side of the mountain with multiple balconies overlooking a spectacular view of the foothills below. The lower level boasted an oversized two-car garage with a smaller third door on one side, presumably for ATVs and snow gear.

One of the garage doors was open, revealing the gleaming white paint of Christie's Jeep Grand Cherokee. As he drove closer, he could see her sitting behind the wheel. Apparently, it was still stalled out.

He feathered his brakes and coasted to a stop in front of her Jeep. In the event he failed to jump start it, he'd have to tow it to the shop.

Killing the motor, he hopped to the pavement, leaving his door ajar.

Christie pushed her door open as he approached. "I'm so sorry to bother you." She looked so stressed that his heart went out to her.

"Do I look like I mind?" He reached her and leaned into the Jeep for a quick hug. "I was hoping to see you again today. Not for this, of course." He waved at the stalled vehicle. "Any idea what's going on?"

"No. It just won't stay running." She shook her head, holding out her key fob to him. "It starts and dies, which is so weird since it drove fine last night. There were no lights left on or doors left open, so I don't think it's the battery."

He'd already ruled out the battery since she'd managed to start the motor. "Here. Let me." He accepted the key fob from her and offered her a hand down so he could slide behind the wheel.

Since he was several inches taller than her, he had to push the seat back. Way back.

She chuckled ruefully as he made the adjustments. "You have a lot longer legs than me."

He flicked a sideways glance down at her legs, liking them exactly the way they were.

"Are you checking me out, Mr. Wakefield?" She stepped closer to him, peering anxiously at the knobs on the dashboard he was fiddling with.

"Yep." He winked at her, then tried to start the Jeep. It flashed to life long enough for him to see what the problem was. Shaking his head, he inwardly debated how to break the news to her.

"What is it?" She worriedly touched his shoulder.

"When was the last time you filled up your gas tank?" He slowly turned his head to meet her gaze, trying to keep a serious face.

"I don't know." She waved a hand. "A week or two ago, maybe? Though I don't put many miles on it, I top it off every time it reaches the half-empty mark." She gave a rueful little laugh. "It was something my dad drummed into my brain years ago."

He wasn't sure what to say to that, since the reading on her dashboard had been clear.

She scanned his expression, then shook her head. "Why are you looking at me like that?"

He was half tempted to claim a loose wire or something to save her pride, but his sense of integrity wouldn't allow him to lie to her. "Your gas tank is empty, babe."

She frowned. "That's not possible! It was..." she paused and adopted a faraway look, "at about the three-quarters full line last night."

Concern gripped him. "You mean when you left the sandwich shop?"

"Yes."

His mind ran over the possibilities. Had her gas tank sprung a leak then?

As he swiveled in her direction, she stepped back to make room for him to hop down. He couldn't resist momentarily resting a hand on her waistline as he did so. She was so incredibly touchable. He leaned down to brush his mouth lightly against her temple. Then he moved past her to squat down beside the gas tank.

Dropping down to all fours, he sniffed the air. Sure enough, there was the faint smell of gasoline fumes. He lowered his head to the ground and peered beneath the undercarriage.

And there it was. A small pool of gasoline formed a dark circle on the otherwise pristine concrete floor. It wasn't nearly enough gasoline to amount to three-quarters of a tank, which meant most of it must have dribbled out on her drive home. She was fortunate she hadn't gotten stranded somewhere on the highway.

He straightened and rose to his feet, dusting his hands as he broke the news to her. "Looks like a gas leak. I'll have to tow it."

"Okay, well...it's under warranty," she assured.

He shot her a crooked grin. "Wouldn't matter if it wasn't. You're dating a mechanic, remember? I gotcha covered."

"And a cop, apparently."

"So, you *did* hear that part." He cocked his head curiously at her. "Wasn't sure with how quickly you fell asleep earlier."

She looked confused. "How long have you been a cop?"

"A while. I was at the police academy while you were in junior high."

"That long ago?" Her look of confusion deepened.

"I'm thirty-five, Christie." It was probably time to get that detail out of the way. "You gotta problem dating older guys?"

"No. Gosh, no! I'm twenty-seven myself." She shook her head, emitting one of those breathy chuckles he liked so much. "I'm just trying to figure out how the cop part of your life fits alongside the mechanic part of your life."

"It's a long story. Maybe we could take it back to my shop." He angled his head at the cab of his tow truck. "I'm more than happy to take a detour to the coffee shop of your choice, if you'd like."

"You've got yourself a deal, officer!"

Grinning at her sassy reference to his police badge, he hooked an arm around her middle to drag her closer. But before he could think of an appropriate comeback, he heard a door open behind them.

A woman's brittle voice demanded, "What's going on in here? And why's there a tow truck parked outside?"

Christie jolted and glanced worriedly over her shoulder. "It's my mother," she hissed. "Probably best if we pretend not to know each other. She doesn't approve of me dating a mechanic."

Wes glanced in bemusement down at the death grip she had on the lapels of his jacket, figuring it was too late for that.

A slender woman stalked down the three short stairs leading from the house to the garage, pausing at the bottom to meet Wes's eye. "You must be the mechanic." The look she gave him was hard, searching, and infused with suspicion.

Apparently, his new girlfriend hadn't exaggerated about her mother being a difficult person.

"Yep." He kept a possessive arm around Christie's waist, silently demonstrating how little her hostility phased him. "I'm Wes Wakefield. Christie's boyfriend." He eyed her body-suit with interest. It was an outfit a person might see during a fashion show in Paris or Milan, not something a middle-aged mom would normally be found wearing in the rustic town of Pinetop.

The faintest of moans slid out of Christie as her mother's mouth tightened in disapproval. "This is my mother, Ruby Hart," she murmured in a strained voice. To her mother, she pleaded, "Be nice!"

Going on gut instinct, Wes thrust a hand in Mrs. Hart's direction.

After staring at it for a pregnant moment, she glided across the garage to press her fingers briefly to his. It was far from a real hand shake. Her movements were surprisingly jumpy and hesitant, like she was afraid of him or something.

"I hear you're a cop." Her tone bordered on accusing.

"A police detective, yes." Since he was no longer working undercover, he saw no reason to keep the truth from her or anyone else. "Not for long, though. I'm in the process of resigning." Since it was the first time they'd met, he was surprised she knew so much about him. His status as a police officer wasn't common knowledge to out-of-towners.

"To be a full-time mechanic, huh?" She didn't sound too impressed.

He shrugged. "I own my own shop." It wasn't something he was ashamed of. Though earning his mechanic certification had initially only been part of his cover story, he'd discovered he enjoyed working on cars. Plus, he made a lot more money being a small business owner than he ever had as a public servant.

"So my daughter says."

"And another shop in Phoenix," he returned evenly, not sure why he bothered telling her that since he wasn't trying to impress her.

"Oh?"

Christie squeezed his arm, forcing his attention back to her. "I, um...have that appointment to get to, remember?"

He had no idea what she was talking about, so he could only assume she was fabricating an excuse to end the current conversation and get going. He was more than happy to indulge her. After being in Ruby Hart's presence for only a handful of minutes, she was already wearing on his nerves.

"Right." He liked the fact that she seemed in no hurry to leave the curl of his arm. "I'll tow you to the shop and have a look at the gas tank while you handle the other thing."

"Why? What's wrong with your gas tank?" Her mother stepped closer to the Jeep, her blue eyes glittering with more curiosity than concern. It was a detail that Wes found odd enough to tuck away for later contemplation.

"I'll figure that out just as soon as I have it in the bay, ma'am." He hoped it was nothing major, but he knew better than to make promises before running a proper set of diagnostics.

"Fine. I'll get my keys and follow you there." Ruby Hart swiveled toward the door leading back inside the house.

"No, you stay and get settled in, Mom." Christie's voice was uncharacteristically firm. "This meeting is something I have to handle alone."

Her mother looked taken aback. "Then how are you going to get home?"

"I'll drive her back," Wes offered.

The grateful look Christie shot him told him he'd again picked up on the right cue from her.

Ruby Hart folded her arms and regarded them irritably.

"Are you sure you don't want me to follow you? It's not like I have anything else planned for this evening." The way she said it made it sound like her daughter's fault, which was odd considering her last-minute visit.

"We're sure." Christie tugged at Wes's arm to get him moving. "We won't be gone long."

Her mother hugged her arms around her middle, looking a little lost in spite of her perfect makeup and brazen choice of outfits. "You said that before the Jeep stalled out. It's going to take even longer now."

Instead of arguing, Christie moved toward her mom to kiss her on the cheek. "Go inside and lock the door behind you," she instructed in a low voice.

While Wes hurried through the steps of hitching her Jeep to his tow truck, his investigative instincts went on full alert. Christie's mother was afraid of something. He was sure of it. He hoped her daughter would be willing to shed some light on it once they were alone.

She watched the door pointedly as her mother returned inside, only turning around after she heard the deadbolt click into place. Drawing a deep breath, she moved toward the passenger side of his tow truck.

Wes reached out to catch her hand and twirl her back in his direction. "Where are you going?" He enjoyed the way her ponytail swung around, lightly slapping against the shoulder of his leather jacket.

"To get in your truck." She tipped her face questioningly up to his.

"This way." Since he was finished hitching her Jeep, he led her to the driver's door, which was still propped open. Lifting her inside, he climbed in after her, resisting the urge to nuzzle the hairline above her ear. She was so incredibly kissable, but he didn't want to move too quickly with her.

She yanked on her seatbelt a little too quickly from its

holder, making it lock in place. "I think it's stuck." She wrinkled her nose uncertainly at him.

It wasn't, but he didn't bother explaining how to fix it. Instead, he reached around her to snap the seatbelt in place, making sure their hands brushed in the process. He both heard and felt her soft intake of air before he leaned away from her once again.

"Thanks." She tangled gazes with him. "For everything."

"No problem. Fixing cars is kind of in my wheelhouse." He winked at her.

"I was also referring to how you treated my mom." Her mouth twisted wryly. "Like I warned you, she's a handful."

He tapped her nose before facing forward to start the ignition. "She struck me as more scared and defensive than anything else."

"Oh, believe me. Being scared of the world at large is yet another one of her endearing features." Christie rolled her eyes. "She's afraid of everything, Wes. Every spider. Every sound. Every shadow. She's always been a bit on the paranoid side, but it got a lot worse after Dad died."

"I'm sorry." He reached for her hand as he released the emergency brake and rolled forward. It dawned on him that she'd never precisely stated what her dad had died of. Whatever it was, it had taken him prematurely, that's for sure.

"Don't be. She's my problem. Not yours." She pulled a remote control out of her pocket and aimed it at the garage to shut the door as they drove away.

He didn't agree one hundred percent with her statement now that they were dating. However, he simply raised her hand to kiss her fingers. Then he changed the subject. "Feel free to ask me anything you want about my career as a police detective. I'm sure you have questions."

She hesitated for a moment. "What brought you to Pinetop?"

It wasn't the question he preferred to start with, but in for a penny. "A friend," he said carefully.

"Is it someone I know?"

"Her name is Tess Navarro. She's married to the guy who runs Christmas Tree Ranch."

"Do you love her?"

Talk about a loaded question! He shot her a puzzled look, wondering where this was coming from. It seemed a little early in their relationship for her to be jealous of anyone in his past.

"I'm sorry." Christie gently disengaged her hand from his. "It's none of my business. I, um...just let my mom climb too far inside my head, I guess. She's really good at doing that."

He made a mental note to circle back to that later. "How did you find out about Tess?"

"I didn't. My mother stopped off in town on her way to my place and played Sherlock Holmes. According to her, you have the makings of a home wrecker."

"Ouch!" A shocked chortle escaped him. "Okay." He propped his arm on the seat behind her and was relieved when she didn't shrink away from his touch. "So, here's the truth about Tess and nothing but the truth, so help me, God."

She giggled, which made him take heart.

"We met while we were both living in Phoenix. She was a waitress at the time. A very poor waitress who drove a clunker of a truck that was on its last leg."

"And you fixed it up," Christie supplied.

"Yeah. Got to know her in the process. She paid me in food from the diner, which is the easiest way to make a guy start crushing on a woman. However, she never saw me that way." He snorted. "She treated me more like a brother than anything else."

Christie bumped her knee against his knee. "Her loss."

He drew a heavy breath. "So, are we good?"

"As long as you have zero interest in adding home wrecker to your resume," she countered softly.

He burst out laughing. "Not even a little." He cupped his hand around her slender shoulder and squeezed for emphasis.

"Good. My mother will be glad to hear it." Her voice was teasing.

He slowed his speed to halt at a stoplight. "What's she got against me?"

"Nothing, other than the fact you're siphoning some of my attention away from her." Christie briefly tipped her head against his shoulder.

"No, for real." He couldn't imagine any parent expecting that of their grown child.

"That's the truth. Like I said, she's difficult."

He wanted to believe her, but his gut told him there was more going on with Ruby Hart than what met the eye.

"She called me in the middle of the night to tell me she needed a place to stay for a few weeks," Christie continued wearily. "She shows up on short notice every few months. It's always a different story. This time, she claims it was a breakup with a boyfriend. I believe he made the mistake of getting down on one knee and proposing."

"Is that all?" Wes mulled that over for a moment. "Because she's exhibiting the behavior of someone who feels threatened."

"I wouldn't try to psycho-analyze her too much. She feels threatened every time someone gets too close to her. It's always been that way." Christie shook her head. "Dad was the only person she ever seemed to fully trust."

"What about you?" He raised his eyebrows at her.

"What about me?"

"Does she trust you?"

"Unfortunately." Christie made a face at him. "I guess that

makes me the second person in the world she trusts. It's a mixed blessing, believe me."

"Why's that," he questioned when she fell silent. The light turned green, and he pressed down on the gas pedal again.

"Because we have absolutely nothing in common. It's hard to believe we're even related. She's a fashion-conscious, label-hunting socialite, forever hoping to catch her big break on the modeling circuit, while I'm the polar opposite. A horse whisperer, content to bum around in jeans during the week and yoga pants on the weekend. My rise up the rodeo charts was strictly by accident. I don't enjoy the spotlight one bit."

"It was no accident," he assured with a quick squeeze hug. "You earned it, babe."

"Thanks." The humble gratitude in Christie's voice made him suspect her mother had gone out of her way to erode her confidence in that fact. He fully intended to do the boyfriend thing and build her back up.

"So she's a model, you say?" That surprised him. With how temperamental her mother was, he couldn't imagine her applying herself to the often grueling schedule of a model.

"That's what she tells her friends. I'm not sure how hard she's trying to land an actual contract. I think she likes the idea of it more than anything else. Other than attending an occasional photo shoot, I'm not sure what else she's done."

He nodded slowly. Her mother was an interesting character. That was for sure. "About that appointment you mentioned, do you need a lift somewhere else?" He feathered his brakes as they reached the parking lot of Pinetop Auto.

"No. I just needed an excuse to get out of the house. My mother sucks up most of the air, so it's harder to breathe around her." She gave a self-deprecatory chuckle. "I have my suitcase packed in the event I need to escape to a hotel."

He backed her Jeep into the auto bay as he digested that last piece of information. Spending more time with his new girlfriend this evening was fine with him. "Feel free to stay as long as you want."

"Thanks." She shot him a grateful smile. "I wouldn't mind finding out what's up with my Jeep before heading back."

Her answer seemed to rule out the possibility of staying for a movie night. *Bummer!* "I'll let you know as soon as I figure it out," he promised.

Both Felipe and the car he'd been working on were gone. No surprise there. The guy never lingered on Saturday evenings. Probably had a social life to get back to. He'd even gone to the trouble of pulling Wes's pickup around to the front of the shop outside. It was thoughtful of him and greatly appreciated. Wes mentally underscored his plan to offer the guy a full-time position soon.

He lowered Christie's Jeep from the tow truck and hooked it up to a diagnostic machine. While he waited for the results, he pulled a mechanic dolly over with the toe of his boot, laid back on it, and rolled beneath the Jeep to take a closer look at the undercarriage.

"Whoa!" He wasn't sure how he'd missed it back in her garage, but the entire skid plate was gone. Christie's gas tank, oil pan, and transmission were completely exposed to the elements.

His gaze latched on to the small, jagged hole in the bottom of her gas tank. It didn't look like something that had been caused by a random bump against a curb or high piece of pavement. Someone had deliberately poked a hole in the lining of the tank.

He pulled out his cell phone and turned on his flashlight app to examine the hole more closely. It could've been caused by any number of objects — possibly a drill with a steel bit. There seemed to be some striations around the lining of the hole that lent credence to that theory. While he was down there, he snapped a few pictures of the damage to send off to a friend in forensics.

Christie was tapping her foot impatiently by the time he resurfaced. "Well? How much is this going to set me back?"

He curled to his feet. "I wasn't planning on charging you. Thought I made that clear."

"Wes, I'm not going to just use you because you're my boyfriend."

He grinned at her choice of words. "Why not?"

"Because I don't make a habit of taking advantage of people. I expect to pay a fair price for a fair—"

He swooped closer to seal his mouth over hers.

She remained still for a moment. Then her arms crept around his neck. "What are you doing?" She tipped her head back to gaze up at him in blushing confusion.

"Accepting fair payment."

"Cute, but this isn't fair to you." Her expression was a little dazed as she reached up to touch his cheek.

"Maybe I like being used by you, Christie Hart."

"Wes," she sighed, tracing the line of his jaw.

He liked the feel of her fingers on his face. It made him wish like crazy that they were on a date, so they could further explore the attraction simmering between them. However, this wasn't a date, and he had some pretty tough news to break to her.

"Your gas tank has been tampered with," he informed her quietly, hoping not to alarm her too much. "I think you should file a police report."

Her face paled. "What do you mean by tampered with?" She dropped her hand from his jaw to his shoulder, as if needing something sturdier to hold on to.

"Your skid plate is missing, and there's a hole in the bottom of your gas tank. Looks like it might've been drilled. Not sure, but I took some pictures. A friend of mine who works in forensics might be able to tell us more about the hole."

She frowned as she tried to process what he was saying. "What's a skid plate?"

"I'll show you." He reached for her hand and led her to his office. For security purposes, it was a windowless room in the back of his shop. It wasn't a place he invited many people into, since he kept two safes there — one carefully concealed beneath the sporty black-and-white checkered tiles under his desk and another behind the false back of his gun cabinet. He knew a thing or two about hiding stuff he didn't want others to find.

Leading her around his red metal desk, he motioned for her to take a seat in his black swivel chair.

She sank weakly into it.

He booted up his computer and pulled up a few pictures of skid plates and explained their function.

"You're right. This was clearly sabotage." Her expression was glum. "Should I call the police, or do you want to do the honors?" She gestured at him. "Since you're, um, one of them?"

He lifted his phone to call the local sheriff's office. He identified himself and where he was calling from. "Gotta vehicle in my shop that's been tampered with. The owner would like to file an incident report."

Sheriff Dean Skelton gave a long, drawn-out sigh. "This was a nice, quiet town before you arrived, Wakefield."

"What are you saying, Sheriff?" Wes didn't consider the recent case he'd assisted the local PD with to be one bit his fault. The guy they'd arrested had followed Tess into town.

Dean ignored the question. "Make and model?"

"Jeep Grand Cherokee, about six months old."

"Did you sweep it for prints?"

"Nope. All I did was take a few pictures." *Isn't that your job?*

"To hang on your wall?" His friend gave a bark of dry laughter.

"You know what I plan to do with them." It was off the record, of course. His friend in forensics owed him a favor. "I'll let you know if anything shakes out."

"Thought you were resigning."

"That's why I called you. Plus, the vehicle belongs to my girlfriend. Don't need any conflict of interest on the record."

"Aha! The plot thickens, as they say in the movies."

"It's Christie Hart." Wes glanced over at her, not wanting to upset her any more than he had to. Her name alone would alert the sheriff to the many possibilities of what they were dealing with — a stalker, a would-be kidnapper, that sort of thing.

"Dang!" He could hear a few things being moved around as the sheriff gathered his gear. "I'll be there in five."

CHAPTER 5: PLAYING CHAUFFEUR

CHRISTIE

It was dark outside by the time the sheriff finished his examination and report. He and Wes conferred in quiet undertones. Then the sheriff took off in his patrol vehicle.

Christie gave a shiver of apprehension as Wes strode around his desk to prop a hip on the corner of it. He reached out a hand to her.

She took it, and he used it to tug her out of his chair. He pulled her closer. "You okay?"

She nodded, trying to think of something to smooth the worry lines from his forehead. "Even though it's sabotage, this isn't my first brush with danger." Attracting stalkers and troublemakers came with her celebrity name and paycheck.

"True, but I imagine you hired a security team while you were on the road." His gaze narrowed on her face while he waited for her answer.

"I did." She heard the question behind his words. "I honestly didn't think it would be necessary in sweet little Pinetop, Arizona. I guess I was wrong." For the first time that day, she was kind of glad her mother was in town. It was probably best not to be alone in her cozy little mountain chalet tonight.

"You sure there's no one in particular you can think of who might want to hurt you?" The sheriff had already covered that question in spades, but Wes didn't sound ready to let it go. "A jealous coworker? A vengeful ex? An overly zealous fan?"

"No, no, and no, detective." She emphasized her answers by lightly tapping a finger against his shoulder with each one. "I appreciate your concern, though. I truly do. But I already told you and the sheriff everything I can think of, and now I really do need to get home. My mother will be jumping at every sound and shadow by this point."

Wes toyed with her fingers. "Any chance you'll let me play the part of your faithful chauffeur for the next few days? Just to be safe?" He purposely dragged her hand across the front of his shirt.

She felt the outline of a holster and a gun strapped there. The gravity in his expression made her smile weakly. "I kind of liked dating a mechanic while it lasted." He was in solid detective mode now.

"We'll get back to that soon." He laced his fingers through hers and raised her hand to kiss her knuckles.

She heard the *I hope* behind his words. "Thank you, Wes." There were so many things she wanted to tell him, but she really did need to get back home soon. "I'm sorry to drag you into my problems." She glanced at the wall behind them. Her Jeep was parked on the other side of it. "I doubt landing a chauffeuring gig was what you had in mind when you asked for an introduction to me."

"I'm not complaining." He held her gaze steadily. "It'll give us a chance to get to know each other better."

"Are you sure you still want to?" She wouldn't blame him if he wanted to tuck tail and run.

"Very sure," he assured tenderly. "In case you haven't figured it out yet, I don't scare easily."

"I'm happy to hear it." She smoothed a hand across his shirt. "Just for the record, I'm not much of a cook." He'd been so nice to her that she figured he deserved a fair warning about one of her biggest shortcomings.

He snorted. "Is that code for something? Because I'm not following you."

"My bad." Her lips twisted wryly. "It's just that there was this smokin' hot cowboy mechanic earlier who mentioned that the quickest way to a man's heart was through his stomach."

"I didn't say that precisely." He grinned at her.

"You heavily implied it."

"Yeah, well, maybe you found another way into my heart."

She liked the sound of that. Keeping their hands laced together, she tugged him away from his desk and walked backwards with him toward the door of his office. "About the sleigh ride you mentioned..." She wondered if he'd mind postponing it until after her mother left town, but he started speaking before she could ask.

"Thanks for the reminder." His expression brightened as they entered the auto bay. "I meant to tell you I was able to schedule it for tomorrow, right after church. I hope that's okay?"

He looked so hopeful that she didn't have the heart to say no. However, he deserved to know what he was up against. "I'm pretty sure my mom will insist on attending church with us in the morning. And, er, she sticks to me like a cocklebur when she's in town."

"Then bring her with you." He tipped his forehead against hers as they continued their slow advance toward her ride home.

He led her to a white pickup parked in front of the shop

outside. She could only assume the tricked out rig with over-sized tires was his personal set of wheels. It certainly looked like something a detailing guy might drive.

"She won't like being a third wheel," she warned, liking the fact that he hadn't hesitated to include her mother. She could only hope he didn't live to regret his kind offer.

"Hopefully, she'll enjoy the scenery despite her third-wheeling." He smoothed a strand of hair back from her face. "I sure plan to."

She got the distinct impression he was no longer referring to the snowy landscape. "Me, too," she murmured shyly, hardly able to believe he was acting so into her. Though she'd daydreamed about him for years, he'd kept his distance from her during her college days.

He reached around her to open the door of his pickup, interrupting her troubled thoughts. Hoisting her inside, he leaped up after her. Gazing at her for a long moment, he muttered huskily, "I like the way you look in here."

"Really?" The question slipped out before she realized what she was saying. At his surprised look, she added, "Listen, I'm still absorbing the fact that I'm dating Bonnie's step-brother."

Caution hooded his gaze. "Is that such a bad thing?"

"You tell me! You barely noticed I existed back then!"

"Not true!" Indignation rang in his voice. "Yeah, I kept my distance, but it wasn't because I didn't notice you. Definitely not that!"

"Oh." She studied him in confusion. "Then, why did you?"

He snorted derisively. "I was twenty-five when we first met. You'd just turned eighteen."

"I remember." A smile tugged at her lips. "You crashed Bonnie's impromptu birthday celebration for me." She'd purchased a small round cake from the grocery store, topped with a decadent amount of buttercream icing, and brought it back to their dorm room for a girls' night in.

"Yeah, she was pretty furious about that."

"You made up for it by ordering pizza for us," she reminded with a chuckle. Then her smile dimmed. "But you didn't stay to eat it with us." He'd left before it arrived.

"Only because my sister booted me from the party."

She frowned at him. "Why?"

"She never approved of my interest in you due to our age difference and all." He raised his eyebrows at her. "Figured you knew that."

"Wait! Back up!" Christie reached blindly for him, curling her fingers around his upper arm. "You were interested in me back then?"

He grinned at her hand on his arm. "Can you think of any other reason a grown man would tag along to so many college football games with his kid sister and her gorgeous roomie?"

"Because you like football?" *You think I'm gorgeous?* A blush warmed her cheeks.

"That wasn't the only reason." He covered her hand with his. "Or even the most important reason."

"Why am I just now hearing about this?" Not once had he shared his feelings with her back then, nor had he made any attempt to ask her out.

"I don't know." He sobered. "I figured you and Bonnie had long since laughed off my hopeless crush on you."

"No. We didn't." She shook her head dazedly. "I honestly had no idea you felt that way about me." She tightened her fingers on his arm. "But you're saying Bonnie did?" She couldn't say why, but it felt like a betrayal.

"Yep, but she made me see the light about just how bad of a boyfriend I would've amounted to." He brushed his fingers back and forth across her hand. "My job would've kept me away from you for weeks at a time. Sometimes months. I wouldn't have been able to romance you the way you deserve. But now I can." His voice grew rough as he gathered her in his arms. "If you'll let me." He pinned her with a gaze full of longing. "Assuming you want this as badly as I do."

"I do want this." She'd wanted it for a very long time.

"I'm going to kiss you unless you stop me," he warned, dipping his head closer to hers.

She had no interest in stopping him. She leaned into his kiss, touching her lips to his.

"Christie," he muttered, reaching up to cup her face. Tracing the skin beneath her lower lip with his thumb, he deepened their kiss.

Every cell in her body felt like it was floating. Dating Wes Wakefield was something she'd fantasized about for years. Actually being in his arms, though, exceeded anything she could've imagined. He was strong, tender, caring, and protective. Finding out he'd been attracted to her for as long as she'd been attracted to him was truly the icing on the cake.

"Wow!" His voice was hoarse by the time he broke off their kiss.

She couldn't have agreed more. Tipping her head against his shoulder, she allowed him to continue holding her while she rode the sea of emotions churning between them. It took a few minutes to catch her breath.

"So, this is really happening," she said dreamily.

"Finally." He tangled a hand in her hair and gave it a light, teasing yank. "It's been a long time coming, don't you think?"

"Yes. I just wish we hadn't taken such a wide, winding path to find each other."

"All in God's perfect timing," he said quietly.

Or maybe God's perfect timing had been delayed because of Bonnie's interference. That part of his story was still troubling Christie. Once upon a time, she and Bonnie had been close — the tell-all-your-girlish-secrets kind of close. That's why it made no sense that she would keep something from her as important as Wes's interest in her.

Christie totally wasn't buying his age difference explanation. She and Bonnie had joked too many times about how they were both attracted to more mature men. Not to mention Bonnie had ultimately married someone several years older than herself.

There had to be another reason Bonnie had run interference between her and Wes. Maybe she'd ask her about it when she finally got around to calling her.

"What are you thinking?" Wes pressed his cheek to the top of her head.

You don't want to know. Christie didn't see any good coming from bad-mouthing Bonnie to him. Maybe she'd find the answers to her questions on her own. Maybe she wouldn't. What mattered most was that she and Wes had finally found their way back to each other.

"A lot of things," she murmured vaguely. "Mostly about how happy I am that you rigged the coin toss on our blind date."

"Half blind date," he reminded, reaching around her to pull on her seatbelt. He clicked it into place for her, then pulled his on.

He pressed another quick kiss to her lips before letting her go.

Christie raised a hand to her mouth as he started the motor, feeling a little guilty over how long she'd been gone from home. Her mom was probably having a complete meltdown by now.

She stared out the window as they cruised down the brilliantly lit Main Street. Though she'd spent most of her life in big cities, the cozy little Christmas town was growing on her. There was just something about the festive window displays that made it feel like home. She wasn't sure what it was.

There were homemade candles, hand-spun taffies, endless baked goods, as well as expertly carved furniture and trinkets. It was a town where pedestrians were often seen walking hand in hand. Tonight was no exception. Happy couples lined both sides of the street. An impromptu group of carolers serenaded them from the gazebo in Town Square.

With a sigh of contentment, Christie reached for Wes's hand. "I like it here in Pinetop," she confessed.

His long fingers laced around hers. "Does that mean you're planning on sticking around?"

"I am." A lot of people had asked her that same question over the past six months. It was the first time she'd been able to give anyone an honest answer. Until her not-so-blind date with him, she hadn't been able to make up her mind.

But now she had.

"Me, too."

She gazed at him in the moonlight. "What about your shop in Phoenix?"

He shrugged. "I'll continue visiting there a couple times per month, but the guy I have running it has a good head for business. The shop's in great hands."

"I'm glad to hear it."

He squeezed her hand. "Any plans to hit the road again on tour?"

"No." There'd been offers, of course. Plenty of them. "My agent isn't too happy about it, but I always pictured retiring at the top of my game. The longer you stay in this biz, the more you risk incurring a career-ending injury." She tipped her head back against the seat cushion. "Nothing lasts forever, Wes."

"I disagree." His voice took on a fervent edge. "According to my Bible, things like faith, hope, and love have a pretty long shelf life."

She wanted to believe him. However, she'd spent way too

much of her adult life waiting for the other boot to drop. It had started with her father's death. Flunking out of college followed. Fast on the heels of those two events was her mother's spiral downward. Unfortunately, Ruby Hart was still spiraling. And despite all of her craziness, Christie dreaded losing her altogether.

"You got quiet all of a sudden." As they reached the empty stretch of highway leading to her chalet, the LED lighting of Wes's undercarriage made the pavement glow purple.

"Do you really believe love lasts forever?" Christie's mother had started dating again a mere two years after her husband had passed. To Christie, it smacked of disloyalty, like watching her parents' thirty years of marriage go up in smoke.

"I do. It's why I don't date much." He slowed the truck to turn into her driveway.

His answer surprised her. "You don't?"

"Nope. Never been a big fan of casual dating."

She caught her breath at the implication of his words. "Me, either. I used to tell myself it was because I was too busy with my career."

"But?" he pressed as he brought his truck to a halt in front of her porch.

The motion detector floodlights kicked on.

"It's more than that." She studied their joined hands resting on his knee. "I've always wanted my words and actions to mean something." She'd overheard too many adults tossing around the L word as casually as they said hi or bye.

"Same with me." He swiveled his head to seek out her gaze beneath the glow of the floodlights. "Every time I hold your hand and every time I kiss you, it matters to me. You hear?"

"You're looking for a serious relationship, huh?" she asked softly.

He reached over to tip her chin up. "I think it's safe to say I'm no longer looking." He punctuated the declaration with a kiss that left her with no doubts that he meant what he said.

ON WES'S DRIVE TO HIS APARTMENT, HE DIALED HIS stepsister. It had been a couple of weeks since his last call to her — too long.

"Hey, Wes!" Bonnie's voice rang affectionately across the line. "How's my favorite undercover mechanic?"

"No longer undercover, for one thing," he returned cheerfully. "I'm resigning, remember?"

"You've been saying that for the past six months." She made a scoffing sound. "Yet you're still tying up loose ends, whatever that's supposed to mean."

"It means I've submitted my resignation, but I'm still doing some consulting on a few ongoing cases." He'd promised to see them through to the end.

"For how long?" she demanded.

"Until we wrap them up or the trail goes cold." He was ready to change the subject. He hadn't called her to talk about work.

"Is it my imagination, or is there a little extra bounce in your voice?"

Now you're talking. He grinned. "I met someone."

She drew a sharp breath. "Tell me *everything!*"

"You know her."

"More," she pleaded. "Quickly! Details, details!"

"Do you remember Christie Hart?"

His stepsister drew a sharp breath. "No. Way."

"I'll take that as a yes."

"Omigosh, Wes! A little build-up next time would be nice before laying a bomb like that on me!"

"Where's the fun in that?" he taunted, thoroughly enjoying her reaction.

She barely stopped to take a breath before demanding, "So, how is Christie, and what's she been up to since she left college?"

"She's a world-class trick rider, living in the town where I work. She accepted a position at a small indoor rodeo here to slow the pace a little. Wouldn't be surprised if she gets inducted into the Rodeo Hall of Fame soon."

His sister gasped. "Are you pulling my leg?"

"Nope, and I'm dating her. Not pulling your leg about that, either."

She was silent for a moment. "This seems a little sudden." He heard what she left unsaid. She was referring to his recent infatuation with Tess. "Not that I'm complaining," she added hastily. "If you're happy, I'm happy."

"Thanks." It was hard to describe how things had ended up with Tess, so he was glad his sister wasn't digging too hard into that. Tess was amazing, no doubt about it, but a romantic relationship between them simply wasn't meant to be. He could see that now. God had different plans in store for him. Plans he was very sure involved Christie Hart.

"Ding, ding, ding! Earth to Wes! We're still talking here!" His sister sounded impatient.

Realizing he must have missed a question or two, he forced himself to tune back in to their conversation. "I'm here. Sorry about that."

"How in the world did you manage to reconnect with my college roomie, of all people?"

"Over a blind date that was only half-blind, since I requested the introduction." She'd have fun mulling over that bit of information. "Plus, I'm serving as her chauffeur for a few days. Her Jeep got vandalized," he explained.

"There's the catch." His sister made a tsk-ing sound.

"You've always been attracted to needy women. Just admit it already."

He smirked at the accusation. He'd heard it before. "No idea what you're talking about."

"Oh, come on! You're a complete sucker for damsels in distress." She sounded disgusted. "Everyone knows it."

And that makes me a bad person? "So I enjoy being needed and wanted. Nothing wrong with that."

"Just promise me you'll be careful, Wes. I don't want to see you get hurt," she sighed. "Again."

They were back to talking about Tess, which he had no interest in doing. It was time to end the call. "I'll be careful." Since he and Tess had never officially dated, his heart hadn't gotten too banged up when it didn't work out between them.

"I wish I was there to keep an eye on you." The sigh remained in his stepsister's voice.

He was kind of glad she wasn't, considering how badly she'd warned him away from Christie in the past. "So, you're cool with me dating Christie this time around?"

"What do you mean?" Bonnie's voice grew strained.

"I'm no longer too old for her or too married to my job to be a decent boyfriend?"

His sister was silent for so long that he assumed she wasn't going to answer the question. When she finally started speaking again, he couldn't have been more surprised by her words.

"Those weren't the real reasons I wanted you to stay away from her, Wes."

"Care to elaborate on that?"

"Not really, but you're not going to let me rest until I do," Bonnie sighed.

"You're right about that. Just say what you have to say and be done with it." He couldn't imagine what bur Bonnie still had under her collar about Christie after all this time, but...

"Her dad was under investigation for some stuff," she admitted in a hushed voice.

"What stuff?"

"I don't have all the details. Dan was the one who told me about it."

"Dan! As in your husband, Dan?" He couldn't believe what he was hearing, because it could only mean one thing — that his stepsister had been intimately involved with her professor-turned-husband much sooner than he'd realized.

"That's the Dan." There was laughter in her voice and a bit of ruefulness. She knew what he was thinking.

"How would he know anything about Christie's father?" Wes scrambled to piece the details together.

"Dan's father was representing the pharmaceutical company in the litigation against her father."

Why does that not surprise me? "So much for attorney-client privilege," he growled. He'd never been a big fan of Evermore & Sons, Attorneys at Law. They had offices in every state in the west and were forever making headlines because of the sensational cases they took on — celebrities, serial killers, you name it. They'd been accused by several prominent watchdog organizations around the country of helping a number of heinous criminals escape justice.

"Dan's not like that, Wes. He was only trying to protect us."

"From what?" She'd always claimed her husband was different from the rest of his family. That was why he'd chosen to teach law instead of practicing it.

"From a guy who allegedly stole a bunch of files from the pharmaceutical firm he was working for."

Wes's insides knotted. "Why would he do that?" Dr. Jimmy Hart had been a research scientist at one of the biggest pharmaceutical firms in the nation. Why would he have felt the need to steal from his own company?

"No idea. It's a secret he took to his grave," she sighed.

"Were the files ever recovered?"

"No. And according to Dan, it's a huge setback since they reportedly contained the formula to a cutting edge vaccine. It could literally take years to replicate the research."

"Good gravy!"

"You can say that again."

Silence settled between them as he mulled over what he'd learned. It was doubtful Christie had the missing files in her possession. Nothing about her actions following her father's death supported that theory. Quitting college and diving headfirst into horse therapy were the actions of a grieving person. Her mother's actions might bear looking into, however, if it ever came to that, which Wes hoped it wouldn't.

Sensing that Bonnie had told him everything she knew, he opted to change the subject. "Christie may be reaching out to you soon." With any luck, the news would perk his sister up. Once a law student and now a stay-at-home mom, she tended to be a little starved for adult conversation. "I gave her your number. Hope that's okay?"

"I can't believe you feel the need to ask. Of course, it's okay! None of that stuff her dad was involved in is her fault, you know," she declared firmly.

"True." He still wished his sister had come clean about Jimmy Hart sooner.

"I'm sorry for keeping this from you, Wes. About Christie's dad and all. In hindsight, I shouldn't have, especially now that you're dating her."

He wasn't sure what she wanted him to say, so he kept silent.

"Am I forgiven, Wes?"

"Yep." He wasn't sure she'd done anything that needed forgiving. Like it or not, she'd only been looking after him when she'd warned him to keep his distance from Christie.

"Thank you. Seriously, though!" Her usual zest for life crept back into her voice. "Your woman is actually a rodeo star?"

"She's at the top of the charts, baby."

"That's just...crazy!" She sounded genuinely glad to learn of Christie's success. "I can't wait to tell Dan!"

He kind of wished she wouldn't since he didn't trust any of the Evermores any further than he could throw them. However, Bonnie was married to the guy, so he was bound to find out eventually.

Bonnie didn't seem to notice that he'd grown silent again. "Who would've thought our paths would cross again after all this time?" Her voice bubbled with happiness.

For him, that was an easy one.

Because God's plans are bigger and better than ours.

CHAPTER 6: SLEIGH RIDE

CHRISTIE

Sunday

"A sleigh ride after church sounds chilly, quite frankly. And I'm not accustomed to being a third wheel." Christie's mother tinkered with the settings on the coffee dispenser. She was overdressed as usual, this time in a three-piece pantsuit that was even more runway worthy than the bodysuit she'd arrived to town in. It was the color of ripe winter berries with a beaded jacket that nearly swept the floor.

"It was Wes's idea." Christie brushed past her in a much more practical gray cable knit turtleneck sweater over a pair of white jeans. Her feet were encased in gray suede ankle boots. "He's hoping for a chance to get to know you better." She watched her mother from beneath her lashes, knowing she'd like the idea of making the sleigh ride about her.

Ruby Hart paused in the middle of loading a peppermint-flavored k-cup. She glanced up to rake her daughter with a speculative look. "He actually said that?" She was fully poised to dislike him, but Christie's words were making her reconsider her position.

"He did." Christie would've preferred to have her new boyfriend all to herself, but his interest in meeting her mother was a good sign. Plus, she had no doubt her mother would choose third wheeling over spending the afternoon alone.

Unfortunately.

It would probably go down in history as the world's most unromantic second date.

Her mother raked her from head to toe, taking in every detail about her outfit. "If that's what you're wearing on the sleigh ride, I might need to go change."

"You look amazing, Mom." She was pretty sure her mother already knew that. "As long as you're warm, I'd keep the suit on."

Her mother preened a little as she puttered with the coffee dispenser some more. She finally lifted her head to pin Christie with a helpless look. "Two things. Will you help me turn this thing on? And do you have a pair of winter boots I can borrow?"

"Yes and yes." Christie took a step back to tap the button for the ten ounce sized coffee. Then she tapped the start button. Steaming coffee trickled into the insulated silver cup her mother had set beneath the spigot.

She set out another insulated cup for herself, preparing to commandeer the coffee dispenser the moment her mother was finished with it. "I'll be right back with the boots."

"Thanks, hon." She waited until Christie was halfway up the stairs before asking, "I know it's a dumb question, since you always tell me no, but—"

"I still haven't found Dad's ring, Mom." It wasn't an outright lie, since it had never been lost in the first place. She paused on the stairs. "I would've thought you'd have filed an insurance claim on it long ago, so why haven't you?"

Her mother waved her hands in agitation. "Because it can't be replaced, hon."

"Sure, it can." Christie pinned her with a scowl. She wasn't sure why her mom was continuing to make such a big deal about it after all this time. "I checked online. The jeweler he bought it from is still in business. I'm sure if we showed them a few pictures, they could easily replicate—"

"No!" Her mother's voice was so sharp that Christie winced. "It wouldn't be the same ring he wore all those years." Her red-painted lips twisted bitterly. "It would look the same, but I would know the difference."

"You're right. I'm sorry." Christie rubbed her thumb over a non-existent spot on the hand railing, still not ready to hand over the last gift her father had given her. Maybe she was being as foolish as her mother for hanging on to it like an emotional lifeline for so long. Maybe she would've felt differently about the ring if her mother had been more generous with Jimmy Hart's other personal effects, but she hadn't. So far, she'd been unwilling to part with a single mug or painting from his office. The ring was seriously the only thing Christie had to remember him by.

"I have a dumb question." She was uncertain how to bring the conversation to a close. "Have you had anyone look inside your floor vents for it?" Though it was a luxury condo, it was an older one full of dated architectural details.

"Of course, I have," her mother spat. "We've taken apart the house, board by board and...nothing."

"I'm sorry," Christie said again. She was mostly sorry they were still talking about the ring, though, not sorry that it remained in her possession. She climbed the next stair, hoping the conversation would end once she was out of sight.

"It's the only reason I've never sold the place," her mother added bleakly, more to herself than Christie. "Or gotten rid of a single dusty old item. That stupid ring has had me stuck solidly in place, unable to move forward." She flung her hands into the air. "Or backward, for that matter."

Christie scowled at her, not liking the vague, unspoken accusation behind her mother's words, as if her failure to move on with her life was somehow her daughter's fault. "I never knew you wanted to sell the condo."

Her mother flicked an angry glance at her. "It's full of nothing but sad memories for me, hon. Hospital beds, endless bottles of medications, nurses coming and going, the scent of disinfectant..." She shook her head sorrowfully. "You wouldn't understand since you were away at college."

"Only because you and Dad never bothered to inform me how bad off he was." A familiar wave of anger swept through Christie, tightening her insides. He'd gone downhill so quickly after he'd gotten sick. His doctor had claimed it was simply one of the billions of unnamed viruses running around the globe.

"We didn't realize how sick he was at first."

"At whatever point you realized it, you should've picked up the phone and called me!" Christie's voice shook indignantly. "I would've come home. No questions asked." Why, oh why, was her mother choosing to pick this particular fight again?

Her mother merely shrugged. "It was his wish to keep you in college. He was very proud of the fact you were studying law."

Christie let out a long-suffering groan. "If you're trying to make me feel bad about my ultimate choice of careers, it's not working."

Her mother's expression was unreadable. "I'd say that's water under the bridge at this point."

Christie shook her head in disgust. "Why do you do that?"

"Do what?" Her mother's face was a portrait of false innocence.

"Come into town once in a blue moon to pick the same old fights with me?"

Her mother's red-painted lips twisted into a smile that didn't reach her eyes. "To be honest, I've been hoping to provoke you into admitting you have the ring that I've been looking for the past seven years."

Christie gaped at her in astonishment. That was a new tactic. She'd give her credit for that. "That's the most ridiculous thing you've accused me of yet!"

"Is it?" Her mother taunted.

"Seriously, Mom? After enduring years of criticism about my hair color, weight, and total lack of style, I guess I assumed you'd finally run out of insults." *Apparently, I was wrong.*

"I'm sorry you've found my every attempt at parenting to be insulting." Her mother's expression took on a haunted cast.

"Parenting? Really? Nice try, but I think we both know you were trying to be insulting." Christie hardened her heart against her mother's expression. "That's on you."

"All I've ever wanted is what's best for you, hon. Someday you'll see that."

"By cutting off my college tuition, eh?" Christie's fingers curled into fists at her sides. She'd not meant to bring that up after all this time. It had just sort of slipped out.

"That was an accident." Her mother's eyes glittered with irritation. She didn't like being called out on stuff. "By the time I realized what I'd done, you'd already quit and moved on to other things."

"And what about slicing me up with your words every chance you get?"

"If you hadn't kept your weight down, you'd have never

become a world-class trick rider," her mother pointed out in a milder tone. "My voice of reason in your ears has propelled you into becoming the best version of you. If you find that insulting, well, don't expect an apology for it."

"What's wrong with a few extra pounds, Mom?" Wes's words were still ringing in her ears, giving her the courage to pound the point home.

Real men can handle a few extra pounds, Christie.

"A lot, actually." Her mother didn't look the least bit repentant for making such a claim. "A few extra pounds are all that stand between someone trying to land a modeling contract. Or a role in a movie. Or, in your case, the ability to successfully balance your entire body off the side of a horse in full gallop for the entertainment of your audience."

"Okay. You win, Mom. A few extra pounds make all the difference in the world." Christie didn't try to keep the bitterness out of her voice as she stalked the rest of the way up the stairs. Nor did she bother turning around, even when her mother started talking again.

Her mother had to raise her voice for it to carry all the way to Christie's bedroom. "Things would get a lot better between us if you'd simply turn over the ring."

Her hands were shaking as she yanked open her closet door and zeroed in on the pair of boots she wanted to lend her mother. It took her a few extra seconds since they weren't in the exact same spot she'd left them. Her entire collection of shoes and boots had been moved around. Instead of the perfect line she'd left them in, they were all sitting at crooked angles.

Come to think of it, her hangers were all resting at odd angles as well. One of her jackets had been unzipped and was about to fall off the hanger.

Her chest grew cold at the realization that her mother

had searched the place, presumably for the all-important signet ring.

Her hand crept inside the pocket of her jeans where it was currently resting. Tears of relief prickled behind her eyelids as her fingers came into contact with it. The metal was warm from being inside her pocket. If she'd believed for a second that handing it over to her mother would improve their relationship, she would've done it in a heartbeat. She was beyond weary of arguing with the woman. But Ruby Hart was as crazy as a dog in a hubcap factory. Her last outburst had proven that beyond a shadow of a doubt.

Snatching up the pair of faux brown leather snow boots, she stalked back to the kitchen and held them out coldly. "Here you go, Mom." The nasty side of her wished she'd brought down her bright purple ones, just so they'd clash with her outfit. Unfortunately, she wasn't mean-spirited enough to think of something like that in advance, much less follow through with it.

"They don't look as horrid as I was expecting." Her mother kicked off her high-heeled pumps and immediately stepped into the boots. "Has it ever occurred to you," she mused, taking an experimental few steps in them, "that the reason you get so angry with me sometimes is because I'm right?"

Christie stared at her for a moment. "About what?" she exploded. Stomping over to the cabinet, she slid her insulated coffee cup beneath the spigot and selected her favorite flavor of coffee to insert in the k-cup holder. It was a nutty caramel blend. The air was soon filled with its soothing scent.

"About you having your dad's signet ring in your possession, for one thing."

Christie let out a long-suffering sigh. *Aaaand we're back to that.* "Why would you think that?"

"Well, you've never outright denied having it."

"I have, but you've always heard what you want to hear." Christie had denied it in at least a dozen different ways. Her mother simply hadn't been willing to let the topic go.

"Plus, it's the only explanation that makes sense." Her mother's voice grew tight with excitement. "Your dad wore that ring everywhere, even in the shower."

"Ew!" Christie muttered.

Her mother ignored her. "He refused to take it off even after hospice was called in. He was wearing it when you went into his room to say your final goodbyes to each other, and he wasn't wearing it afterward," she concluded triumphantly.

Christie snorted in derision. "You're really obsessed with that ring, aren't you?"

"You would be, too, if you knew what was on it." Ruby Hart paled and grew abruptly silent.

Christie got the distinct impression she'd said more than she meant to. She waited a moment, before asking, "Are we just going to pretend you didn't say that, or are you going to tell me what you meant by it?" Removing her cup from the dispenser, she squeezed a liberal amount of her favorite sugar-free chocolate syrup into it, then finished filling the cup to the brim with sugar-free chocolate caramel creamer. Pressing the lid on, she turned around to face her mother, leaning back against the kitchen cabinet.

Her mother gave an uncomfortable bounce in her borrowed boots. "What do you know about the accusations against your father?"

Christie's heart squeezed painfully as she bent her head over the insulated cup of coffee to breathe in the warm, damp tendrils of steam rising from the open part of the lid. "Only what was in the news. They claimed he copied some files from work."

"Stole them," her mother corrected fiercely. "Leaving no copies for the firm who'd paid millions of dollars to produce said research. It was a coordinated media campaign against him — designed to convince the world he was a low-level thief."

Christie shook her head. "Dad would never do something like that."

"Not for personal gain, no. But I can personally vouch for the fact that he would've gone to extraordinary lengths to protect those he loved." Her voice grew bleak.

"Protect us from what?" Christie demanded.

"You said *us*." Her mother's expression momentarily softened. "I'm almost surprised you included me in that comment."

"He loved you, Mom." Some days, Christie wondered what he'd seen in her mother's insanity, but it was true. "I never doubted it."

"But you never understood why, huh?" Her mother's voice was wry.

"I didn't say that." *Are you a mind-reader now?* It was a scary thought.

"You didn't have to, hon." Ruby Hart paced in a circle around the bar. "I know our relationship has always been a rocky one, but it hasn't been for lack of trying on my part. If only you knew the sacrifices I've made to be your mother."

It was such an odd statement that Christie didn't know how to respond. After a moment of inner debate, she circled back to the topic of the ring. "I'm starting to feel like dad's missing ring is the real reason for your visit, so how about you cut to the chase and tell me why?"

Her mother paused on the other side of the bar, leaning forward to rest her elbows conversationally on it. "It's not the only reason. Believe it or not, I really was missing you."

Christie made a scoffing sound. "You have no idea how badly I want to believe that."

Her mother's smile held a note of triumph. "Fine. You

win. I'll tell you what you want to know, and maybe you'll finally give me what I'm asking for."

Christie gave her an exasperated look. "Or you'll finally admit you're barking up the wrong tree and leave me alone."

"I don't think so." Her mother's smile disappeared. "So, here's what's going on. I have reason to believe that the files your father took from the lab are on his signet ring."

Christie swung her coffee cup around to drop it on the cabinet behind her. "On the ring?" she repeated carefully. "How?" Visions of tiny pieces of microfilm flitted through her head.

"A few days ago, I found a receipt from the jewelry firm where he bought the ring," her mother announced coolly. "I was clearing some things out of his office to donate to charity."

Really? Christie had to swallow her bile over that bit of information. *You refuse to share a single memento with me, but you're gonna just give stuff away to complete strangers?*

"It was wedged so tightly into the corner of the shredder tines that I almost missed it." She paused dramatically.

"Almost missed what?" Christie asked tightly.

"That your dad had done something to the ring that cost more than the original price of the ring."

Christie shrugged. "Okaaay." She wasn't following whatever point her mother was trying to make.

"I did a little research online and discovered that this same jewelry firm specializes in novelty upgrades."

"Such as?" Christie wondered why her mother was making her drag every detail out of her.

"Ring drives, among other things."

Christie frowned as she processed the possibilities. "Are you trying to tell me there's a memory drive embedded in Dad's ring?"

"It makes sense, doesn't it?"

"I'm not sure anything makes sense anymore," Christie muttered.

"It would certainly explain why a creep with a metal detector showed up outside my condo the next day. He was dressed like the meter reader guy, but I know what I saw."

"Mom!" Christie's brain felt like it was going to explode.

"It also means my online activity was being monitored. You and I are being watched, Christie. I always knew we were. I just never had proof until now."

"Why would anyone be watching us?" Christie had never bought into her mother's many conspiracy theories.

"Because of the ring!" Her mother gave her a piteous look. "If anyone even suspected you had it in your possession..."

Christie weighed her mother's words, hating to admit that they made her sound a little less crazy than before. "What will you do with the ring if we ever find it?" She still wasn't ready to admit that she had it.

"Destroy it!" The fact that her mother didn't even hesitate struck her as strange.

"Why not turn it over to the police?"

"If it was that easy, I imagine your father would've already done it."

She gave her mom a helpless look, knowing her father was, hands down, the smartest guy she'd ever met. "Then I guess we'd better find that ring."

Before her mother could answer, a knock sounded on the front door.

Relief coursed through Christie at the realization that Wes had arrived. "That's our ride to church." She was more than ready for a break from all her mother's doom and gloom talk.

As she jogged to the front door to pull it open, her mother called after her, "This conversation isn't over!"

The moment Wes stepped inside, Christie flung her arms around his neck. "Am I ever glad to see you," she breathed.

There were snowflakes clinging to his jacket and Stetson. He swept his hat off to brush his mouth against hers in a toasty kiss. "That sounded like a loaded statement." He spoke quietly against her lips. "One I'll be asking for an explanation for later."

"Please do," she whispered back, anxious to share all the new information her mother had piled on her this morning. "Just wait until we're alone."

"Okay." He rubbed a thumb across her lower lip, looking like he wanted to say more. However, he merely clapped his hat back on his head, probing her with his dark, all-seeing gaze as he helped her into her gray wool coat.

"Morning, Mrs. Hart." He finally turned to face her mother, who'd silently joined them in the foyer.

"Hello, Wes." The raking look she gave him made Christie groan inwardly. "Since my daughter has warned me to be on my best behavior, I'm not even going to ask why you prefer the life of a mechanic over that of a police detective."

"Like my warning did any good!" Christie's voice was faint.

Wes merely chuckled. "I'm ready to pursue a few other dreams." He gave Christie a pointed look that made her blush.

"I take it my daughter is one of those dreams?" Ruby looked pleased when Wes hurried to her side to assist her with her jacket next.

"Yes, ma'am."

"Can't say that I mind the thought of a cop looking after her." She swept out ahead of them to the front porch. "Good gracious!" She stopped short, clasping her gloved hands tightly around her insulated cup of coffee.

"Now what?" Christie murmured, hurrying after her. On

the porch, she stopped short beside her mother, curling her fingers around her own cup of coffee. It appeared there'd been a change of travel plans.

The shiny red sleigh Wes had promised to ride them around town in after church was parked on the snow covered driveway in front of her chalet. Six absolutely lovely draft horses were stamping their hooves, impatient to be moving again. Their stout bodies were covered in glossy, reddish-brown coats, and their legs were drenched in long white hair. It fluffed over their hooves like the cuffs of bell-bottom pants.

"You mean you didn't know about this?" It was impossible to tell what her mother was thinking as she continued staring at the horses.

"Will it do any good to claim my innocence?" Christie chuckled wryly as she turned around to lock the front door after Wes. "It's not like you're in the habit of taking me at my word." She rolled her eyes for his benefit.

She turned around in time to see the skin around her mother's mouth tighten. "I would if you were telling the truth, which you are this time."

Wes stepped between them, reaching for their arms to bustle them down the porch stairs. "I hope you ladies don't mind joining me for a sleigh ride both to and from church. Flash had a cancellation this morning, which doesn't happen often, so I grabbed the opening."

As they reached the sleigh, he gestured at their driver, an older gentleman dressed as Santa. "This is Flash Billings, our faithful postmaster and sleigh driver. He also plays Santa at all the town parties."

"I don't know what you mean about playing!" Flash tipped his red cowboy hat at them. "I'll have you know this beard is real."

"Flash, this is my girlfriend, Christie Hart, and her mother, Ruby Hart. She's visiting from Dallas."

"We all know who Christie Hart is, son." Flash made a tsk-ing sound as he met Ruby's gaze. "It's just like these young fellers to sweep into town and steal the prettiest girls out from beneath the rest of our noses."

Wes's eyebrows rose. "I wasn't aware you were on the hunt for another, er, Mrs. Santa."

"Didn't say that I was," the older gentleman informed him cheerfully. "Though I occasionally run into a lovely lady who makes me want to rethink my widower status." He winked brazenly at Christie's mother.

Christie wasn't sure whether to laugh or groan as she braced herself for the set-down her mother was sure to give him.

Instead, she was forced to listen to her mother's titter of appreciation. "If that's an invitation to join you up front, I'm accepting." With a gleeful look in her daughter's direction, she stepped boldly up to him. Holding out a hand, she beckoned imperiously for Flash to help swing her up beside him. "Anything is better than sitting in the back, playing third wheel to these two lovebirds."

"Well, that worked out better than expected," Wes rumbled low in Christie's ear.

In the next moment, he was lifting her onto the rear bench like she weighed no more than a feather and climbing in after her. He tugged a lap blanket over them. "Are you warm enough?"

"I'm getting there." She tipped her head against his hard shoulder, loving the gentle glide of the runners beneath them as they took off.

He slid his arms around her. "Now?"

"Better," she burrowed closer.

"How about now?" He nuzzled her cheek.

"Perfect." She turned her face to brush her lips against his. "So, what do you know about ring drives?"

He chuckled quietly against her lips. "You sure know how to keep a guy on his toes."

"Pretend we're necking," she instructed in a breathless voice. "I don't want my mother to know we're having this conversation."

"There's no pretending." His voice was husky as he swooped in for another kiss. "The way I feel about you is very, very real, Christie Hart."

She reveled in the eager drag of his lips against hers. "The feeling is mutual, Mr. Wakefield." She hated the necessity of tainting the moment with yet another one of Ruby Hart's conspiracy theories. However, if she and her mother were truly being watched, Wes had a right to know what he was getting into. "About what I asked..."

"There aren't many ring drives in circulation. Most folks, quite frankly, aren't trying that hard to hide anything."

She shivered and lifted her insulated coffee cup between them to take a sip. She positioned it to hide the lower half of her face from her mother and Flash as she continued talking. "My mother seems to think my father had his signet ring altered to hold a drive, presumably to hide the files he took from the lab where he worked."

"Allegedly took." Wes tipped up the coffee cup she pressed to his lips and took a swig.

"Thanks for giving him the benefit of the doubt."

"You make the best coffee." He pressed the cup back into her hands.

"Thank you."

"I'm going to go out on a limb here and speculate that you know something about the whereabouts of this infamous ring." He cuddled her closer again, tipping her mouth up to his as he spoke.

"My mother said the same thing," she whispered nervously. "I'm not sure why you both jumped to the same conclusion."

"I have a degree in kinesics." He nipped at her lips. "That means I can hear pretty much everything folks leave unsaid."

"Uh-oh." Her voice grew shaky. "If I say yes, are you going to turn me in?" Because of his badge, would he be legally obligated to do so?

"What kind of boyfriend do you take me for?" He looked incensed.

"The kind who's probably feeling caught between a rock and a hard place about now."

"I'm Team Christie all the way." He flicked his thumb over her chin, his gaze returning hungrily to her mouth. "Don't you ever doubt that."

"Oh, my lands!" Her mother's dramatic exclamation made their heads spin in her direction.

Ruby Hart leaned closer to Flash as they passed a scraggly-looking hiker.

Flash tipped his head at the guy.

He nodded back and continued trudging through the snow.

"Normally I would've stopped to offer the fellow a ride." Flash shot Mrs. Hart a curious look.

"Who is he?" Her voice was hoarse.

"Some groupie who showed up for Christie's first rodeo performance." He shrugged. "He's been here ever since."

Her mother stiffened at his explanation and tossed Christie what could only be described as an I-told-you-so look.

"It's okay, Mom. He's not the first rabid fan I've had, and he won't be the last." Christie wasn't surprised that her mother was jumping to the worst possible scenario.

"Then explain this," her mother demanded huffily. "The

last time I laid eyes on that bum was early in the summer. Down at the beach house in Florida. He was combing the sand with a metal detector."

Christie exchanged an uncertain look with Wes. "How can you be sure it was the same guy?"

"If he has a birthmark on the underside of his chin that looks like a chocolate milk stain, then he's the same guy," her mother insisted darkly.

"The fellow does seem to be hovering." Wes's eyebrows scrunched together in concern.

Ruby Hart twisted anxiously around in her seat. "Do you know something I don't know?"

"He was sitting in the booth next to Christie and me during our first date," he supplied.

Christie couldn't believe he was propping a crutch under her mother's paranoia. For a guy who'd majored in kinesics, he should know better than to feed that beast. "Are you even listening to yourselves? None of the things you mentioned make that scraggly little hiker back there anything more than a Christie Hart fan. I have them, you know. Lots of them!"

Nervously pushing back his bright red hat, Flash jumped back into the conversation. "This is probably the right time to confess that I've seen the underside of that fellow's chin, and he does have a brown birthmark there."

Three sets of eyes bored holes into his festive red suit.

"Caught 'em pushing a metal detector around Christie's chalet yesterday. I set him straight real quick on the sacredness of property lines around Pinetop."

Looking utterly defeated, Ruby Hart slumped down in her seat.

Christie's hand crept to the ring in her pocket. Pushing one gloved finger through it, she curled it in her fist and pulled it out. Under the guise of hugging Wes, she dropped it into his left coat pocket.

He tipped his forehead against hers. "Did you just...?"

"It's the last thing my father gave me before he died, Wes. That's the only reason I've refused to part with it all these years. I'd never even heard of ring drives before Mom brought them up this morning."

His gaze glowed into hers. "The fact that you trust me with this means more than I can say."

She shivered, more than a little afraid of what she was dragging him into.

CHAPTER 7: COMING HOME TO ROOST

CHRISTIE

A week and a half later

C hristie could hear Wes's truck rumble into her driveway. She glanced at the digital clock on the stove. He was earlier than usual by a good twenty minutes.

As she hurriedly finished mixing creamers in coffees, the thought crossed her mind that this morning might be the perfect time to place that long-anticipated call to Bonnie. She'd sort of been dragging her heels on it. However, she couldn't avoid talking to her former college roomie forever, especially now that she was dating her stepbrother.

That is...unless Wes had deliberately carved out some extra time to spend with her, in which case she'd be giving him all twenty of those extra minutes.

Her mother slunk into the room, her platinum blonde hair poking in all directions. "Boy, you leave earlier and earlier each day," she grumbled.

"Good morning, Mom." Christie slid one of the mugs of

coffee her mother's way. "Two fingers of creamer, exactly how you like it."

"Thanks, hon." In an uncharacteristic move, her mother briefly squeezed Christie's fingers before curling her hand around the mug. "In case I haven't said it yet, I appreciate you letting me stay here. I wasn't sure where else to go after..." Her words dwindled to silence as she took her first sip of coffee.

Christie inwardly finished the sentence for her. *After you gave in to your latest bout of paranoia.* She wished there was something she could do to convince her mother that the whole world wasn't out to get them. She was really hoping that Wes's forensics contact would find no memory drive on the ring. Maybe after she received confirmation of that, she'd finally come clean with her mother about having the ring in her possession. She still wasn't sure she'd ever be able to part with it, but she didn't want to continue lying about it.

She hurried to the entry foyer to grab her favorite red swing coat from the hall tree. Before opening the front door, she twirled back to her mother. "You're my mom," she declared impulsively. "You don't need a reason for visiting, and you're always welcome to stay as long as you want."

Unless it was a trick of the light, her mother blinked back tears as she tipped her head over her coffee. "I love you, Christie. Don't you ever doubt it."

"I know you do, and I love you right back." Sometimes, Christie feared it was the only middle ground the two of them shared. For the first time in a long time, however, it felt like it was enough.

"Tell Wes I said to drive safe," her mother added sharply.

"He will." Despite his juiced-up set of wheels, he never played games on the road. Every once in a while, one of the younger guys in town tried to coax him into a drag race, but he always waved them on.

"I know you feel like nothing bad can happen to you inside his mammoth truck, but what I see rolling out of your driveway every morning is all the family I've got left."

Christie paused with her hand resting on the door handle. "Sheesh, Mom! If you wanted a hug, all you had to do was ask." She moved back across the room in her snow boots to throw her arms around her mother's slender shoulders.

"Thank you." Ruby Hart was too busy trying not to spill her coffee to hug her back, but the warmth in her voice was better than a hug.

"As soon as Wes gets my Jeep back up and running, we'll do lunch, okay?"

Her mother gave her a quick up-down nod and followed Christie silently across the room to lock the door behind her.

Christie waited on the front porch until she heard the deadbolt fall into place. It was their mother-daughter morning ritual that seemed to give her mother comfort.

Wes revved his motor playfully as she reached the bottom of the stairs, making her feel the rumbling vibrations. It was seriously the coolest truck. Its extra wide tires and all the other upgrades made it look as macho as its driver. It didn't explain why her SUV was still sitting in his shop, though. A week and a half seemed like a long time to replace a simple skid plate, but what did she know? Maybe he had to order the part or something.

As he jumped to the ground to assist her into the cab, she handed him the cup of coffee she made him every morning. She might not be much of a cook, but she could hold her own when it came to brewing a decent mug of coffee.

"Thanks." He hooked an arm around her middle and dragged her closer for a good morning kiss. Then he gave her a hand into the cab. "You take such good care of me."

"I try." Her heart sang at the heavy-lidded look he gave her. He was into her, as in *really* into her. She didn't need a degree in kinesics to figure that out. Her womanly intuition was firing on all cylinders when it came to anything involving Wes Wakefield.

He glanced away from her as he took his place behind the wheel, his jaw working as he slammed the door shut. "Christie, I don't know how to say this…"

She held her breath, wondering if he was about to drop the L word on her.

"Your mother was right about your dad's ring. It's holding a memory drive."

Her heart sank at the unwelcome news. "And?"

"There are some pretty incriminating files on it."

"Making him look guilty, I presume?"

"Not him." Wes reached for her hand to lace his fingers through hers.

She shook her head, thoroughly perplexed. "I'm almost afraid to ask who."

"He doesn't give their names. He simply refers to them as a rogue set of investors. According to his notes, they were forcing your father and other scientists on his team to create a number of mutated versions of the same deadly virus."

It felt like all the air was leaving her lungs. "Why would anyone do that?"

He shrugged as he backed out of her driveway. "Your guess is as good as mine. They were also tasked with developing a top-secret vaccine."

She frowned. "For a set of viruses they were creating?"

"Looks like. The rogue group of investors poured millions of dollars into a series of overseas shell companies to fund the research."

She shook her head. "I may have only completed my first two years of a pre-law degree, but even I can tell you that's not how pharmaceutical research is normally conducted."

"That is correct."

She stared blindly out the window at the passing snow-drifts, wondering how her quiet little life in the cozy town of Pinetop had turned into such a nightmare. A mere hour ago she'd been shopping for a new bedroom set online — one with a king-sized bed and a reclinable mattress that had a bazillion and one massage settings built into it.

"There's more," Wes informed her gently.

"Of course, there is." Her voice was bitter.

"Apparently, someone in the lab was accidentally exposed to one of the viruses, so the untested vaccine was adminis-tered off the books. There was a ton of paperwork signed to indemnify the lab before the vaccine was given." He cast a worried look in her direction. "I'll give you one guess as to who signed all the paperwork."

"I take it we're discussing someone I know?"

"Yes."

A sick feeling pooled in her stomach. "Dad?"

"Bingo."

"Who was the patient?"

"So far, I've been unable to locate a name anywhere in the files."

"So, did the vaccine work?"

"I haven't yet found that information, either. This could take a while, though. There are a lot of files, and I'm no scientist."

"You said *you* can't find it," she repeated numbly. Why was he the one examining the ring drive? "I thought you said some guy in forensics owed you a favor."

"He still does."

Because you never called it in. She gulped as her thoughts tumbled dizzily one over the other. "You never passed the ring off to your buddy, then?"

"No."

"Because?"

"This is potentially a lot bigger than us, Christie."

"But you're a cop!" Anger surged through her over his duplicity. She tried to pull her hand away from his, but he held it tighter. "Aren't you legally obligated to turn this information over to...I don't know...somebody?"

"Not anymore." He lifted her wiggling hand to his lips. "I turned in my badge before I started reading the contents of the zip drive. That's why it took me a week and a half to get back to you with an answer."

"Oh, Wes!" She sank weakly back against the seat cushion. "Did you seriously quit the force for me?"

"I was already planning on leaving," he reminded. "I simply sped up the timeline a little."

"A little?"

He shrugged. "It could've taken months or even years to wrap up the rest of my caseload. I didn't need any wrinkles in those cases pulling me away from you. Nor did I wish to be bound by oath to report whatever I found on your father's drive to the authorities."

It became harder to breathe as the seriousness of the situation sank into her. "My mother is convinced I have the ring drive. She came into town for the express purpose of hounding me into turning it over to her."

"Did she say what she plans to do with it?"

"Yes. She intends to destroy it."

"Maybe that's not such a bad idea."

"Wow! So that's it?" She wasn't sure why, but it felt anticlimactic to let things end like this. She still had so many unanswered questions burning inside her, and she still wanted justice for her father. There was no doubt in her mind that he was innocent.

"It's not my call, Christie. But I'll say this. I learned a long time ago that you can't solve every case or collar every bad guy. In too many cases, the bad guys have better lawyers."

"Like Evermore & Sons," she supplied bitterly.

"Yeah." His jaw hardened.

"Okay, then. I have one last request to make."

"Anything." He lifted her hand to his lips again as he pulled into the rear parking lot at Castellano's.

"Help me break the news about all of this to my mom, please."

He parked the truck and turned to face her, pinching her chin to tip her face up to his. "Just to be clear, you're asking me to be present when you finally confess to having the ring in your possession all this time?"

"Yes."

"When?"

"How about tonight over dinner?"

"I can do that." He dropped his hand.

"Good." She glanced at the clock on his dashboard.

He followed her gaze. "Got somewhere better to be, Miss Hart?"

"Better? No." She slid her arms around his neck. "But I still haven't called your sister, and she's probably wondering why I haven't."

He hitched her closer. "I reckon that's a halfway decent reason to let you head inside to work early."

"Only halfway?" she scoffed.

"Maybe not even that." He claimed her lips, showing her just how reluctant he was to say goodbye.

She dragged her gloved fingers through the back of his hair. "I miss you already."

He chuckled against her lips. "What time do you want me to pick you up?"

"Would five-thirty be too early? I know you have a shop to run."

"I own the place, so I can come and go anytime I want." When she started to protest, he pressed a finger over her lips.

"Plus, I offered Felipe a full-time position yesterday, and he said yes."

"I'm so happy to hear it, Wes!" She drank in his joyous grin, knowing how badly he'd been wanting to bring on a full-time mechanic with him at his shop. "This feels like something we should celebrate."

"I agree." He lightly tapped her nose. "Good thing my girl invited me over for dinner."

"In case you're worried about your stomach lining," she added quickly, "my mom is cooking."

"I wasn't the one who was worried." He leaned in to brush his mouth over hers.

"Unlike me, she's an incredible cook," she promised.

"Doesn't matter." He kissed her again. "I promise to eat anything you cook me in the future. Burnt toast or whatever."

She pretended to sock him in the gut, and he pretended to suck in an oomph of air.

"I do *not* burn my toast, thank you very much."

"Good to know." He grinned at her.

"Seriously, Wes! You just toss the bread slices into the toaster and push the button. Even I can't screw that up."

"If I agree with you, are you going to punch me again?"

As she playfully drew back her fist, he wrestled her for it. She ended up imprisoned in his embrace.

"Man, Christie!" He pressed his cheek to hers. "I'm falling so hard for you. I hope it's okay to admit that."

"The feeling is mutual," she whispered. Her heart was too full to say more.

"Good," he said huskily, stealing another kiss before letting her go. "If you plan on calling my sister, you'd better make a run for it." He pushed open his truck door.

"Thank you, Wes. For everything." She was a little in awe of all he was doing to help her and her mother.

"There's nothing I wouldn't do for you, Christie." He touched her cheek.

When she swayed in his direction again, he hopped to the ground and reached for her to pull her down beside him. Then he gave her a gentle push toward the back entrance of the dinner theater. "If you let me kiss you again, I can guarantee there won't be any time left for you to call Bonnie."

"Alright." Chuckling, she forced herself to march toward the back entrance to Castellano's. The whimsical, red-painted door never failed to make her smile. At the last second, she turned around and blew Wes a kiss.

He was watching her with one hand propped on his open truck door, looking like every single one of her dreams come true in his black jeans and black leather jacket. He swiped the air with one hand, as if catching her kiss, and pressed it to his lips.

With a sigh of sheer happiness, she let herself inside the building. She didn't have an office in the back of the building where the administrative offices were located. Instead, Angel and Willa Castellano had given her the sole use of one of the dressing rooms beneath the center stage. It wasn't that they were being stingy with their space. They simply considered it more secure for a celebrity of her caliber, and she agreed.

Angel glanced up from his desk as she passed by his office. "Morning, Christie!"

"Morning, boss!"

"I thought I told you not to call me that."

"Yeah, well, we don't always get what we want," she teased, though she was fairly certain he usually did. He was a wildly successful businessman and chef, who demanded a lot from his staff. However, he did it with a brand of kindness and generosity that was rare. And no one worked harder than he did.

She made her way to her private dressing room, locking

the door behind her like she always did. She'd been allowed to decorate it anyway she wanted, so she'd made it her home away from home.

All of her tack was stored on hooks and shelves against the wall — stirrups, bridles, halters, reins, bits and harnesses. Her saddles were stacked on extender shelves that went straight up to the ceiling in one corner. In the opposite corner was a brown leather easy chair where she sat to pull on her riding boots. Beside it, a ladder bookcase leaned against the wall. She even had her own beverage station, complete with a coffee maker.

Instead of donning her riding gear and heading straight for the horse stalls, she plopped down in the easy chair and pulled out her cell phone. There was no point in putting it off any longer. It was time to call her college roommate.

Bonnie answered on the first ring. "Omigosh! It's really you, isn't it?"

She sounded so much like the fun-loving girl Christie had once shared a room with that some of the tension left her shoulders. "The one and only Christie Hart," she agreed with a dry laugh. "How are you, Bonnie?"

"Older and married with a mom bod." Her former roomie's voice was equally dry.

Christie wasn't sure what a mom bod was, so she wasn't touching that. "Yeah, Wes told me you have a kid. How old?"

Bonnie made a soft humming sound. When she started speaking again, her voice was muffled. "You wanna tell Miss Christie how old you are, baby?"

"Yes," a young voice shouted in return.

"Here you go, then. Tell her how old you are."

"Tree!"

As soon as Bonnie returned to the line, she asked, "Boy or girl?"

"Oh, he's one hundred percent chip off the ol' block. You were speaking to Dan Evermore, Junior."

"You sound happy," Christie noted softly. "I'm glad."

"Why do I hear a *but* in your voice?"

"There's no *but*," Christie assured hastily. "It sounds like you're living all of your dreams, right down to marrying a mature, older guy."

"If this is about me warning Wes away from you, I'm as sorry as I can be about that."

"You are?" Christie's insides chilled as she waited for an explanation.

"Yes! It was completely wrong of me," her friend exploded. "So wrong. It seriously can't get any wronger."

A reluctant chuckle escaped Christie over the humorously humble admission. "So wrong," she agreed. "I don't know why I'm laughing."

"Maybe because you love me enough to forgive me?" Bonnie waited a beat before adding, "I hope?"

"I want to." Christie fought to swallow the lump of bitterness in her throat, wondering if it was possible to move on from there. Bonnie's actions had kept her and Wes apart for seven achingly long and lonely years.

"There's the *but*," her friend noted sadly.

"Yeah."

"Would it help if I told you that Wes believes your Pinetop reunion happened in God's perfect timing?"

Christie smiled. "That sounds like something he would say."

"I know, right?" There was a sigh in Bonnie's voice. "He's a man of tremendous, unshakable faith. I've come to rely on him in ways I couldn't possibly give up." She was silent for a moment. "That's my way of saying you have to forgive me before you marry him, because I'm never going to stop needing my brother in my life."

"Marry him!" Christie choked out the words.

"It's going to happen. Mark my words," Bonnie assured her in a fierce voice. "There's no way your paths would've crossed again like this if it wasn't meant to be. He adored you back then, and I made the mistake of thinking it was a passing crush. I was wrong."

"Did he, um, say all of that to you?"

"He didn't have to. I could hear it in his voice. During his last phone call, my lonely stepbrother was gone. In his place was the biggest love-sick fool I've ever met."

"Bonnie!" A shocked chuckle eased out of Christie.

"He'd probably shoot me if he heard me saying that, but it's true. I don't know what you did to that boy in the short time you've been dating, but you have him completely wrapped. Nice going, you!"

"Guess we're both living our dreams, huh?" It was the closest Christie could come to saying she'd forgiven her friend.

"If you mean we snagged the hearts of the two hunkiest men in the west, then yes."

"I really care for him, Bonnie."

"I know you do, sweetie. I just wish I'd realized that seven years ago. I am so, so, sooooo sorry that I didn't."

"Okay, I forgive you." How could she not?

Bonnie's answering chuckle turned damp with emotion. "Thank you. I really needed to hear that from you."

There was a murmur of voices in the background. "I gotta run," she said quickly. "One of Dan's brothers texted earlier to say he was in town and wanted to stop by for breakfast." She drew a deep breath. "And here he is."

"Okay, um...bye!"

"Bye." Bonnie ended their call as quickly as it had begun.

Christie was left smiling in bemusement at the phone in her hands. She dreamily reached for the boots on the hook to her right and tugged them on. She grabbed her favorite trick saddle on her way out the door.

Roman Rios, who was quickly becoming her favorite wrangler, tipped his Stetson at her as she sauntered down the hallway between the horse stalls. After her first date with Wes, she now understood that the shadows in his eyes were born of grief.

"Prancer has been pacing his stall for any sight or sound of you."

"Thanks for looking after him." She gave him her brightest smile.

"It's my job, Christie."

She started to walk away, then paused. She'd been desperate to clear the air between them for days. Spinning around to face him, she murmured, "Roman, I'm so sorry about—"

He held up a hand to stop her. "You don't owe me any apologies."

"I just didn't want you to think I haven't rescheduled our dinner because I'm too stuck up to date a wrangler." As soon as the words left her mouth, she blushed in mortification. "Ugh! That sounded better inside my head."

"We're good," he assured. "Or were...until your crack about dating a lowly wrangler."

"I didn't mean that the way it sounded."

"I know." He winked at her. "Just couldn't resist roasting you a little."

"I deserved that." She wrinkled her nose shamefacedly at him.

"Not even. You're one of the nicest women I've ever met."

She let out a sigh of relief. Then she chuckled.

"What?" He smirked at her.

"If I'm one of the nicest women you've ever met, should I

be offended that *you* didn't work a little harder to reschedule our date?"

"Not unless you want to see Wes Wakefield flatten me to the pavement."

Her eyes widened. "What are you talking about?"

"You mean he didn't tell you?"

"Tell me what?" she asked suspiciously.

"Ha! He pretty much ordered my sister to take her match-making skills on a hike."

"Did he really?"

"Naw! He was much nicer about it than that. Still, he made it pretty clear that he wasn't interested in a bunch of competition from yours truly."

Christie liked the way his smile chased away some of the shadows in his eyes. "You're an amazing man who deserves an amazing gal at your side." She bit her lower lip, hoping he wasn't offended by that. "When you're ready, of course."

He sobered. "Sounds like Wes told you I already had an amazing gal at my side once."

"He did." She nodded sadly. "I'm so sorry for your loss, Roman."

"Thanks." He reached for her saddle. "Now that we're no longer stepping on eggshells around each other, how about you let me get back to doing my job?"

She gratefully relinquished the saddle into his capable hands. Moments later, she tried not to be jealous at the way Prancer nickered up a storm while he saddled him.

"Wow! He really likes you. He only talks to people that he likes."

"Again, getting horses to like me is kind of my job, Christie." Roman gave her a mocking bow. Then he cupped his bare hands to give her a lift.

"Thanks." She swung into the saddle, squeezing his shoulder gratefully on the way up.

"My pleasure." The teasing way he waggled his dark eyebrows at her was like getting a peek at the guy he used to be. Before the tragedy. When he was ready to step back into the world of dating, he was going to make hearts flutter for sure.

She could feel his gaze on her as she entered the indoor rodeo ring and broke into a canter. Amphitheater seating rose on all sides around her. The stage that normally anchored the center of the room had been dismantled and stored away. Several layers of special mats had been placed end-to-end across the crisscross of hardwood and tile flooring. A layer of turf had been added on top of them. Angel Castellano had spared no expense in building his indoor rodeo grounds. They'd been designed with the safety of both the animals and their riders in mind.

Christie circled the ring a few times, letting Prancer burn off some of the steam he'd built up overnight in his stall. Only after he settled into his usual rhythm did she crouch on top of her saddle with her knees bent in front of her. In one quick move, she curled upward, bracing her feet on either side of the pommel. With the reins gripped in one hand, she arched her back into the horse's movements and waved at the invisible audience.

The few stage workers broke into cheers, clapping loudly as she rode past them. Though it wasn't the size of audience Prancer was accustomed to, he tossed his head excitedly in response. He thrived on the appreciation of their onlookers.

She circled the ring again, dropping her reins as she did so. This time, she waved with both hands, using nothing but her feet to maintain her balance on the back of her horse.

CHAPTER 8: SILENT
SPECTATOR

DAN

Dan Evermore kept his hat pulled low over his eyes as he hung over the railing. He'd positioned himself in the darkest corner of the amphitheater, hoping no one would notice him.

His father's voice crackled to life in the earpiece he was wearing. "You got your eyes on her yet, son?"

"Yep." Dan was careful to keep his answers short and hill-billy like he'd been coached. He was hoping if he completed his latest field assignment for the family firm, they'd leave him alone for another few months. All he wanted to do was return home to his wife and son.

"According to my clients, either Christie or her mother are in possession of the missing files."

"If you say so." Dan didn't bother hiding his sarcasm. His dad's latest clients sounded like a bunch of whack jobs to him. He definitely didn't like the fact that they had one of his wife's friends in their crosshairs, a woman who just so happened to be dating his brother-in-law. Though it was perfectly legal to be paid to watch some-one, he was tempted to break ranks and warn her. Something about his father's clients simply wasn't setting well in his gut.

"I do say so." His father's voice grew hard. "There was a time when you wouldn't have questioned me about something this important. The kind of research my clients have been conducting at their firm could change the course of history. If you can't see that, then being in the classroom has made you soft."

Whatever. Dan's ears had been filled for years with his father and brothers' insults over his choice of careers. Their words hardly phased him anymore. "Being a softie puts me at your disposal for assignments like this," he reminded in a mocking voice. None of his three attorney brothers could be bothered with something as lowly as a stakeout. They considered it beneath their Italian silk suits, leather wingtips, and gold pinkie rings.

"True. I guess you still have your uses."

"You guess?" Dan snorted. *I'm the only son out here, breathing rodeo dust and doing your dirty work.*

"Did you remember to turn on your video feed?" his father barked irritably.

"Is the sky blue?" The recording device was attached to the second-to-top button on Dan's plaid shirt.

"Not in San Francisco," his father grumbled. "It looks like the apocalypse out here."

Right. Dan had all but forgotten about the latest cloud of smoke covering the sun where his father and brothers lived. The result had been several days of falling ash and glowing orange skies.

"You should visit your favorite grandson more often." He knew his choice of words would rankle since his father had no less than eight grandsons. "We have clearer skies in Stanford."

"Good idea. That's why I sent Benjie to pay Bonnie and Dan Junior a visit this morning."

Dan stiffened, wondering why this was the first he was hearing about his oldest brother's impromptu visit. He was sure it was no accident that it was happening while he was away. He was equally sure that his father intended it to come across as a threat.

"Hopefully, he's enjoying the fresh air." It was difficult, but Dan kept his voice nonchalant. "Kind of hate it that I'm missing his visit."

It was a lie, one that his father didn't grace with a retort. Everyone in the family knew he and Benjie royally despised each other. Most of them mistakenly assumed it was because Benjie had purposely two-timed Dan's high school sweetheart, which couldn't have been further from the truth. Dan was oddly grateful to him for exposing her fickleness before he'd made the mistake of putting a ring on her finger. What he objected to the most about his oldest brother was the blackness of his heart. He would sell out their own mother if that's what it took to close a case. He wasn't sure if their father realized that. He hoped he figured it out before it was too late.

Since Dan was stuck on a stakeout, he figured he might as well make the most of the unticketed show unfolding before him. Christie Hart was everything the tabloids claimed she was — strong, agile, talented, and full of vivacity. Never before had he seen a horse and its rider move in such perfect harmony.

"I need you to get closer to Christie," his father instructed.

"No can do. Not without getting trampled," Dan joked, knowing that's not what he meant.

"Very funny," his father muttered, sounding distracted. No doubt he was glued to the video feed pouring onto his computer from Dan's hidden cam. "I'm thinking more along the lines of you and my daughter-in-law paying a visit to her old college roommate. That way you can poke around, ask some questions, and get a better feel for the situation."

"That'll make my wife happy." He wondered exactly what sort of intelligence his father hoped to gain from such a visit.

While he waited to hear the rest of his marching orders, he mulled over what he knew about the case. It was flimsy at best. He wasn't swallowing the pharmaceutical company's claim that Jimmy Hart had set their research back decades by the files he'd allegedly stolen. There was no way a company that big or that profitable wouldn't have a backup system in place for their files. There had to be more to the story.

The most plausible theory he'd been able to come up with was that Jimmy Hart had stumbled across something incriminating for the firm — a statutes violation, unauthorized clinical trials, or something along those lines.

"Bonnie will join you in Pinetop by the end of the day," his father announced tersely. "At which time, the two of you will pay a visit to Christie Hart. I don't really care what you give as your reasons for popping in unannounced. Just get close to her and report back everything you can."

Dan curled his upper lip. "An all-expenses-paid vacation. I like it." He intended to stick it to his father by letting his wife make liberal use of the Evermore & Son's credit card he had in his pocket. No doubt Bonnie and her friend would schedule a shopping spree or two in downtown Pinetop. He could further annoy his family by purchasing holiday gifts for all of them. It would be hilarious watching their expressions as they opened them on Christmas morning.

"That's why Benjie stopped by your home for breakfast this morning," his father continued in a breezy voice. "Not only did he drop off Bonnie's plane ticket, he's fetching Dan Junior back for that long overdue visit with his Paw Paw that you've been harping about."

Dan's blood chilled at the realization that his father was

basically holding his grandson hostage until his youngest, least favorite son agreed to do his bidding. As infuriating as it was, Dan didn't harbor any real fear for his son's safety. Family meant too much to Benjamin Evermore, Senior. It might very well be his only redeeming quality.

What his father failed to realize was that Dan wasn't the softie the rest of his family mistakenly assumed he was. Far from it. And the emotions his father's latest threat was stirring in him were anything but soft. The man had crossed a serious line by paying an unscheduled visit to Bonnie, then sweeping their son away for an unauthorized trip to San Francisco. She was probably half out of her mind with worry. Dan couldn't wait to have her back in his arms so he could assure her that everything was going to be alright. Eventually.

The lovely trick rider in the ring in front of him pushed her feet into the air, forming a perfect handstand on the back of her galloping horse. As he watched her, he felt an inexplicable surge of protectiveness. For the first time since he'd been dragged to the current stakeout against his will, he was glad he was the son who'd been chosen for the task.

Over his dead body was he going to stand by idly and watch any harm come to such an amazing human being. Not for any amount of money. Certainly not for any misplaced loyalty to the family who hated him.

He'd waited for years for an opportunity to unravel the evil Evermore empire. This might be his one and only chance. No way was he going to pass it up.

BONNIE STARED AT THE BOARDING PASS IN HER HAND. NOT only had her father-in-law personally engineered the removal of her son from her home, he'd already checked her and two suitcases onto her flight. It was due to leave in less than two hours. She'd yet to start packing.

Benjie Evermore was noisily scarfing down the breakfast burritos she'd prepared for him, eyeing her with no small amount of glee. He thought he'd won this round, and he had.

She didn't have to give him the satisfaction of knowing it, though.

"Would you like me to stir up another skillet of scrambled eggs for you?" she inquired sweetly. "I truly owe you for this unexpected gift." She clutched the plane ticket to her chest, giving him her most winning smile. "It's not often a stay-at-home mom gets handed an expenses-paid vacation out of the blue." The effort to hold her smile in place nearly made her gag, but she was pretty sure she pulled it off by the way his oversized jowls tightened with displeasure.

"This isn't a vacation." He tossed his napkin on his plate, eyeing her with suspicion as he ran a hand through his longish black hair. He looked so much like Dan and yet so much *not* like Dan. He was an inch or two taller, much wider, and a whole lot meaner.

She waved a hand playfully at him. "Tomato. To-mah-to. You try staying home all day long with a three-year-old. Trust me. Any break would feel like a vacation to you, too."

"You should hire a nanny," he scoffed. "Not sure why Dan is being so cheap."

Though her insides tightened with rage at the insult to her husband, she gave a scoffing chuckle. "Who needs a nanny when I have an amazing brother-in-law like you?" She stretched and muffled a yawn. "I can't believe you showed up when I was needing a few days off the most. It's like you had your Bonnie radar turned on or something."

"Bonnie radar?" He looked so perplexed that it was all she could do not to burst out laughing.

"Yep. It's really a thing," she assured cheerfully. "If you don't believe me, just ask Dan."

"Think I'll pass." His tone grew bored as he picked a speck of lint from the sleeve of his blazer and dropped it on the floor.

"Your loss, mister. While you contemplate it, I'll get a bag packed for peejinks over there." She didn't dare look directly at Dan Junior, who was happily building a train on the other side of the living room. If she had, she would've burst into tears.

"Don't bother. Mom has everything she needs on hand to care for one more grandkid." Benjie stretched his legs lazily in front of him, crossing his feet at the ankles. The movement made her new dining room chair creak alarmingly beneath his ample weight.

To avoid curling her lip at his hideous mint green paisley socks, she hurried toward the stairs. "I'm sure she does," she called merrily over her shoulder, "but you'll still need your uncle survival kit for the trip there."

Benjie uncrossed and recrossed his feet uncertainly. "What's an uncle survival kit?"

She paused on the stairwell to tick the list off her fingers. "Pullups in case he has an accident, a change of clothes for the same reason, his favorite snacks to keep him happy, his favorite pet dinosaur, wet wipes for..." She giggled. "As a father of three, I'm sure you're well aware of how messy a three-year-old can be."

Benjie glared at her. "You mean he's not yet potty trained?"

"Of course, he's potty trained!" She pretended to recoil in defense. "What kind of mother do you take me for?"

When Benjie didn't answer, she continued to babble. "Not to worry. He only has accidents when he's sick. Or upset about something. Or really tired."

"Is that all?" Benjie's glare deepened.

"You tell me." She gave him her best annoyed look, which was the easiest fake expression to pull off yet. "You've got a lot more dad experience than I have mom experience."

"I seriously doubt it." His bored tone was back. His upper lip curled as he examined his fingernails. "Exactly how big is this pet dinosaur?"

Chuckling, Bonnie bounced up the last few stairs and disappeared into her son's bedroom.

Keep it together, BonBon!

She was two snaps away from dissolving into a raging fit of tears. Never before had she felt so helpless. So out of control. So angry. Drawing a few gasping breaths, she blinked rapidly to dry her burning eyes. Later. She would shed her tears later all over her husband's broad shoulders. But for now, she had to hold them in.

Don't you dare give that rat downstairs the satisfaction of breaking you!

CHAPTER 9: UNEXPECTED GUESTS

WES

Wes could feel Ruby Hart watching him as she pulled a pot roast out of the oven.

His mouth watered as the scent of meat, onion rings, and baked vegetables filled Christie's chalet. However, he didn't let the delectable aroma slow his careful sweep of the room with the debugging device in his hand. He was scanning every electrical outlet, air vent, nook, and cranny where someone might've hidden a camera or a listening device.

"The house is clean," Mrs. Hart announced as calmly as if they were discussing something like the weather. "I already swept it for bugs."

He paused his scan of the central air vent directly over his head. "That isn't a skill you'd normally find on a modeling resume."

"You're right. It's not. Like you, though, I've occasionally required a cover story. Hence, you're a mechanic, and I'm a model." The bleak set to her mouth told him she was telling the truth. Though his detective training called for completing the sweep, his gut told him that she cared too much about her daughter's safety to lie about something so important.

As a sign of trust that he could only hope wasn't misplaced in her, he lowered his arm and pocketed the scanning device. With any luck, the gesture might buy him a few brownie points with her. He was nearly finished with his scan of the main floor, anyway. She had to have known that, which begged the question as to why she'd waited so long to halt his progress.

"I appreciate everything you're doing for Christie," she continued as she carried the platter to the center of the table and plopped it on top of a pair of quilted hot pads. "She wrote me off as a loony tune a long time ago, but she listens to you. For that, I am more grateful than you will ever know."

"I know you're not her biological mother." He'd read enough of the contents of the memory drive to start piecing together some very interesting details about Ruby Hart's past. "Does she?" He glanced up at the second floor where Christie had gone to change out of her riding gear and take a quick shower.

"No." Ruby Hart grew deathly pale. "I'm not going to ask how you found out, but I am going to ask that you keep it that way as long as possible. Ignorance is not simply bliss in this case, detective. It's what's keeping her alive."

Though he nodded, he wasn't sure he agreed with her statement. Not only was knowledge power, keeping secrets from the woman he was dating felt like a recipe for disaster.

"You've looked out for her at a tremendous sacrifice to yourself." He hadn't understood the lengths she'd gone to protect her niece until he'd finished deciphering another file on the drive only hours earlier. He'd been holed up in his office at the back of the auto body shop all afternoon.

"And I would do it again in a heartbeat," Mrs. Hart

declared fiercely. "My husband was worth it, and so is she. I love her like she's my own."

"She loves you, too." Wes was sure of it, but he sensed she could use a little convincing.

"I know, and it's the craziest thing. She thinks I'm a hard-hearted, self-centered freak, yet she found a place in her big beautiful heart for me, anyway."

"Of course, she did. You're her mother."

Her face scrunched up. "The closest thing she's got to one, I suppose."

"You're her mother," he repeated firmly.

Four hours earlier

A POCKET OF TURBULENCE ROCKED THE AIRPLANE, MAKING Bonnie squeeze her armrests in a death grip. In a stroke of irony, there'd been a mix-up with her seat assignment, so she'd been moved to the first-class cabin.

The extra complimentary beverage before take-off had been nice. However, none of the perks of flying first class amounted to a hill of beans now that the plane was descending. Of all the things in the world that she hated, flying was at the tippy-top of her list. She'd never been one hundred percent sure why — if it was caused by her fear of heights, a touch of claustrophobia, or a combination of the two.

Her breathing grew shorter, until it was reduced to short gasps. They flew through another pocket of turbulence that made the whole plane shudder and sway from side to side. Bonnie squeezed her eyelids shut, trying to grit her way through the final minutes of the flight.

Less than twenty minutes now.

In an attempt to distract herself, she whispered one of

her favorite verses from the Book of Psalms. "If I ascend to heaven, You are there. If I lie down with the dead, You are there. If I rise on the wings of the dawn, if I settle by the farthest sea, even there Your hand will guide me..."

The next patch of turbulence was even more violent than the first two. She experienced the sensation of being batted around the sky like a tennis ball. Tears trickled out from beneath her eyelids.

If I ascend to heaven, You are there.

Her lips were too numb to speak the next line aloud, so she continued reciting it in her head.

If I lie down with the dead...

Though she understood the faith being expressed by those words, she knew with sudden certainty that she wasn't ready to die. Her son still needed her, and she had too much unfinished business yet — not the least of which was reclaiming her little family from the grasp of the hateful Evermores.

"Are you okay, ma'am?" The gentleman sitting next to her patted her shoulder.

"I'm fine," she fibbed, feeling anything but. "I'm just ready to be back on the ground."

"We're almost there," he assured kindly. "We're only a hop, skip, and a jump away from landing."

Please stop talking! Though the man meant well, nothing he said was going to talk her out of her fear of flying. She was going to remain a miserable basket case until they reached the ground.

Either she spaced out, or they were closer to landing than she'd realized. All she knew was that the wheels of the plane touched down on the runway. She was thrown back in her seat as the wing spoilers went up and the pilot laid on the disc brakes.

"See? What did I tell you?" The older gentleman chortled happily.

"You were right." She opened her eyes that she'd kept shut for the remainder of their descent.

"Is someone going to be at the gate to greet you?"

"Yes. My husband." Just saying those words aloud brought a sense of peace to her like nothing else could.

Her hands trembled as she reached for her cell phone and turned off the airplane mode. A flood of text messages peppered her screen, along with notifications of a few missed calls.

A text from Dan was waiting for her. Three simple words.

I love you.

More tears trickled down her cheeks, making the gentleman next to her glance her way worriedly again. She avoided making eye contact with him, knowing it would be impossible to explain that they were tears of relief this time. Unless he had an airplane-phobic wife or girlfriend some-where in the world, there was no way she could make him understand.

The moment the plane came to a halt at the gate and the seatbelt light flashed off, she was on her feet. She kept her head down, wiping at her face with the backs of both hands as she exited the airplane.

"Have a nice day!" The stewardesses waved and twittered like birds at the front of the cabin.

Bonnie was too embarrassed to look up as she trudged past them. She was mostly just grateful that she'd never see any of these people again.

When she left the secure area, there was such a large crowd milling on the other side of the gate that she couldn't immediately locate her husband. Her head spun from left to right.

Then his strong arms closed around her.

"Bonnie!" Dan's raspy baritone rumbled against her ear.

She sank joyfully into his embrace, resting her head against his muscular chest. Though he was in his late thirties, he still put in an hour at the gym at least four days per week, usually five, and sometimes six. He jokingly claimed he did it because he had a young wife to impress.

"You found me," she sighed.

"I always will, babe." His lips found her swollen ones. "Tough flight, eh?"

She thought she was done crying, but his empathy made her eyes well again. "It felt like a bucket of rusty bolts about to fly apart on the way down," she grumbled as more tears slipped and slid down her cheeks. "Sorry. I'm such a horrible flyer." She reached up to brush them away, but he slid his hands beneath hers.

"My turn." The pads of his thumbs rubbed a gentle circle against her cheeks, easing the tension in her facial muscles she hadn't even realized was there.

He leaned in to kiss her forehead, the tip of her nose, and each damp cheek. Then he pressed his face to the side of her neck, just breathing her in.

She threaded her fingers through his dark hair to hold him there for a moment, both needing the comfort he offered while hating that he was seeing her at her worst.

"Never again will my family put you through something like this," he declared fiercely as he raised his head to latch onto her gaze. "You have my word."

"Thank you. I'm still sorry that I'm such a coward when it comes to heights," she muttered. She was married to a man who would happily take her anywhere in the world — Paris, Rome, Fiji — but all she wanted was to be back home, tripping over Dan Junior's toys and counting the minutes until Dan made it back for dinner.

"Baloney!"

She gaped at him.

"Cowards tuck tail and run. Brave people stare their fears in the eye and meet them head on. That's what you did, baby. I couldn't be prouder of you."

"I love you so much for saying that." She cuddled closer to his strength and the scent of his arctic ice aftershave that she could never get enough of.

"You're my whole world, Bonnie. You and Dan Junior." He swooped in to nuzzle her earlobe.

"About our son," she intoned softly.

His expression was black with anger as he raised his head to meet her gaze again. "That's something else that will never, ever happen again." There was something so final about his words that she shivered. "I've been more than patient. More than a dutiful son. To be treated like the black sheep of some mafia family in return is unacceptable. I will be making that very clear. Very soon. On my terms."

Trying to lighten the mood, she offered, "I was just going to let you know that I sent Benjie away with a whole package of pull-ups that I guaranteed he would need to use if our son was tired, scared, or upset. Then I threw in a big pack of wet wipes and the messiest snacks in the pantry to ensure he'd get to use plenty of those as well. As a parting gift, I sent the two of them out the door with the pet dinosaur." It was over four feet tall. The sight of Benjie scowling his way out the door with it tucked under his arm had been truly satisfying.

Dan whistled long and low beneath his breath. "He had no idea who he was messing with."

"Oh, and I thanked him profusely for the unexpected break that stay-at-home moms like me don't get very often."

Dan's gaze darkened with guilt. Before he could apologize for the long hours he sometimes worked, she pressed her fingers to his lips. "What he didn't understand was that I'm not looking for a break from you or Dan Junior. Like you, the only thing I'm looking for is retribution."

"I've already got our rental car reserved, babe. Things are about to get exciting in Pinetop." He sealed the promise with a kiss that made her heart feel like it was soaring higher than the rickety little airplane had only minutes earlier. Smooth sailing this time. No turbulence.

CHAPTER 10: THE SAFE ROOM
WES

Christie joined her mother and Wes at the dining room table, her damp blonde hair smelling of vanilla and honeysuckle. No sooner did she take a seat than a knock sounded on the front door.

Wes half rose from his chair. "Were you expecting someone?"

"No." She stood and moved toward the door. "I'll see who it is."

"I'll go with you." He unbuttoned one of the middle buttons on his plaid shirt and reached for the gun he kept strapped to his chest.

"Good gracious, Wes!" She eyed the gun in his hand. "You can't just go all G.I. Joe on us and start shooting people!"

"Watch me." He kept his expression deadpan just to tease her.

Ruby called his bluff by chuckling, "I like this guy."

"Wes," Christie pleaded softly as she stepped closer to the peep hole.

"No G.I. Joe moves," he agreed silkily. "Just for the record, I never fire my weapon unless it's a life or death situation."

She gave a squeal of excitement and reached for his hand. "It's Bonnie!"

"You've got to be kidding!" He nudged her aside to take a peek. "And her husband, Dan." He frowned. "This is a little unexpected."

"I don't care what it is." Christie was already unlocking the door and pulling it open. "Bonnie!" She held her arms out to her friend.

Wes was dismayed to note how puffy and red-rimmed his stepsister's eyes were.

Catching his upraised eyebrows, Dan explained, "Turbulent flight."

Wes's eyebrows remained up. He was surprised to hear that anyone had gotten Bonnie on an airplane. She passionately hated flying.

As the two women chatted a mile per minute, Ruby Hart waved their group back to the dining room table. "I hope you brought your appetites. There's plenty of pot roast for everyone."

"I'm so hungry I almost took a bite out of the service station attendant a few minutes ago," Dan admitted with a grin. He rubbed his belly for emphasis.

Dinner passed in a flurry of college stories and more than one jibe at Bonnie for eloping with her professor.

Wes watched Dan closely, but he neither acted guilty nor took the bait. He kept an arm propped across the back of his wife's chair, drumming his fingers lightly on her shoulder. There was no mistaking the adoration in his eyes.

Wes was forced to revise his concerns about their marriage. Dan wasn't the source of his stepsister's ongoing unhappiness. Something else was weighing on them both. He could see the strain around their eyes and the hard set to Dan's jaw.

"So how's Dan Junior?" Wes finally asked. He was a little

surprised that neither Bonnie nor Dan had brought him up yet in conversation. He was even more surprised that Bonnie had been coaxed into parting with him. To Wes's knowledge, it was the first time she'd ever left her son overnight.

His question was met with a pained silence. Then Bonnie's eyes grew glassy with unshed tears.

"He's, er, visiting with his grandparents," she announced brightly — too brightly.

Wes's suspicions were instantly aroused, making him wonder if one or both of them were wearing a wire. His sister sure seemed to be going out of her way to warn him.

"Their generosity is what made this trip possible," she added in the same falsely bright tone.

It was all Wes could do not to roll his eyes. Dan could well afford to take his family on vacation anywhere he wanted, anytime he wanted. And Wes was willing to bet that Pinetop wasn't on any of his lists of desired destinations.

Dan shrugged offhandedly, slightly turning in his chair to face him.

That was when Wes noticed his earbud. He tried not to stare at it as Dan continued speaking, "What can I say? My father got wind of Bonnie reconnecting with a long-lost college friend, and he couldn't resist speeding up their reunion. What an old softie, eh?"

By now, Wes was very sure that something was wrong. Though he didn't know Dan extremely well, Bonnie had made it very clear on more than one occasion that her father-in-law possessed the temperament of a Tyrannosaurus Rex. An old softie he was not! Wes would grill his sister about it the moment he got her alone.

In the meantime, he attempted to channel the conversation back to a lighter note by shooting her a wicked look. "If no one else is going to mention the elephant in the room..."

"Which one?" She spread her hands mockingly. "How you

managed to land a date with the biggest rodeo champion in the west or—"

"Nah, I'm sure Christie is more interested in hearing how you managed to elope with your favorite law professor."

She burst out laughing, and the strain lines around her eyes smoothed out. "He's an attorney." She waved airily at her husband. "They know things."

"What can I say?" Dan spread his hands. "The moment she walked into my classroom, I knew my days as a single guy were numbered. We waited until she completely unenrolled from the university, of course, before we, er..."

"Eloped?" Wes shot them a mocking look.

"Basically, yes." Bonnie blushed to the roots of her chestnut hair.

"Why does it feel like you're skipping a few details between her promenade into your classroom and your ride off into the sunset together?"

To his delight, Bonnie squirmed in her seat. "I'm so going to get even with you for this," she hissed.

"Bring it on, darlin'."

"Fine. You and Christie." She gestured at both of them. "First date. Details."

Christie crinkled her eyes at the memory. "It was a blind date, actually."

"Half blind date," Wes corrected with a smirk. He slung an arm around Christie's shoulders and leaned closer to stage whisper, "That's why we corroborated our story in advance, babe. Changing it during an interrogation makes us look like we have something to hide." They were seated directly across the table from Bonnie and Dan. Mrs. Hart was holding down the head of the table to his right.

"How about a game of cards or dominoes?" she inquired suddenly. "Back when my husband was alive, we used to play a game after nearly every dinner. It was the perfect time to visit and swap stories about our day."

"I'm game! Are you?" Christie glanced his way for confirmation.

"Sure. Why not?" He was fine just visiting, but her smile told him her mother's suggestion had jogged a happy memory.

Bonnie nodded eagerly, elbowing her husband, who waggled his eyebrows playfully at her. "Fair warning. We're pretty competitive when it comes to games."

"Duly noted." Wes pretended to stretch and pop his knuckles.

Dan leaned forward and announced casually, "That's my wife's way of saying you should prepare to lose."

Mrs. Hart pushed back her chair. "Alright then." She reached for the bread basket and carried it to the kitchen. When she returned, it was empty. "All cell phones and electronic devices are off from this moment forward. That's the first rule of family games. No exceptions," she added in a severe voice as she passed the basket around the table.

"Just do what she says." Christie rolled her eyes. "She inherited one of those wand thingies from my dad, the kind they use in airport security lines. Suffice to say, if you're hiding any electronics, she'll find them."

"And confiscate them until the end of the game," her mother added in the same no-nonsense tone.

Dan abruptly stood. "If someone will point me to the restroom? I've gotta make one last call. Then I'll hand everything over when I return."

Christie's mom pointed the way to him. Then she actually produced the aforementioned wand, looking supremely satisfied with herself. "In case anyone thought I was kidding..." She tapped it lightly against her hand.

"I'm totally clean now that you have my cell phone."

Bonnie waved her hands in surrender. "Dan wasn't. That's what he's taking care of right now. No wand will be necessary, though, I promise."

"As I suspected." Mrs. Hart tapped the wand against her hand again. "All that talk about the wand was for the benefit of whoever was listening." She grimaced. "Or watching."

Bonnie ducked her head guiltily.

Wes shook his head in surprise at her and mouthed, *What is going on?*

She dipped her head closer. "I'll tell you later."

Mrs. Hart picked up the basket of devices she'd collected from them. "I'll lock them away while we finish our discussion in the safe room."

Christie blinked in astonishment at her. "What safe room?"

"I'll show you as soon as Dan gets back."

Dan returned to the table with a grave expression. "I'm not sure if my earpiece can be turned on remotely, so I left it on the cabinet in the bathroom with the light off and the exhaust fan on."

"Perfect." Mrs. Hart looked satisfied. "Now follow me." She led them to the entry foyer. In one swift motion, she rolled aside one of the dark wood panels. One moment, they were facing a solid wall. In the next moment, they were facing a narrow stairwell leading down.

She instructed the last person to roll the wall closed behind their group. At the bottom of the stairs was a silver steel door secured by a control panel with a number pad. She punched in a six-digit code, and the silver door swung open, revealing the promised safe room.

"This is unbelievable!" Christie gave a twirl inside the spacious subterranean room, taking it all in. It resembled a cozy second living room or den with bookcases, overstuffed leather furniture, a gaming table, and shelves of survival gear.

There was even a Christmas tree in the far corner, glimmering with strands of tiny white lights.

By Wes's best estimate, they were standing behind the two-and-a-half car garage. The safe room might even share the rear concrete wall of the garage.

"How did you know about this, and I didn't?" Christie spun back to her mother.

"Let's just say it was no random slice of luck that you found this particular chalet to purchase, hon." Ruby Hart spread the arms of her creamy sweater wide. She'd paired it with berry colored jeans and ridiculously high-heeled boots. "After you insisted on moving to this snoozy little mountain town, I called in a favor with a realtor who knew a realtor in this town." Her smile grew pensive. "If trouble ever followed you here, I wanted you to have a safe place to run to."

Christie studied Ruby Hart as if she was seeing her for the first time. "This is truly amazing, Mom. I have so many questions to ask, but first..." She nodded at Wes.

He nodded back and beckoned their group to take a seat around the game table. Instead of reaching for the deck of cards or box of dominoes in the center of it, however, he met their gazes one by one. "Pow wow time."

"Please keep an open mind about what you're about to hear," Christie pleaded, "because what Wes is about to tell you is going to require you to think outside the box. In some of our cases, waaaay outside the box." She sent a laughing look at her mother.

"You mean me?" Her mother sounded surprised.

"I didn't mean it as an insult. We both know there's not a spontaneous bone in your body." Christie waved a hand at her. "You like your coffee one way only, and you follow a strict diet. Plus, every hair is always in place, and every sock is always folded away with its perfect mate. You're steady. Reliable."

"I think the word you're hunting for is predictable," her mother supplied witheringly.

"If the shoe fits," Christie teased.

"What if it doesn't?" Ruby Hart lifted her chin. Wes watched as she warred with herself over what to say next.

"I wasn't trying to pick a fight."

"I know." Her mother squared her shoulders. "But you think you know me, and you don't. It just goes to show how deceiving appearances can be."

Christie watched her in wide-eyed fascination. "How so?"

"For starters, I'm not who you think I am."

"I think you're my mom." Christie's voice was soothing.

"I want to be, and I've certainly tried to be."

Christie's lips parted in confusion.

"The truth is, I've been playing a role with you for a very long time. I had myself convinced it was the only way to keep you safe from some very dangerous people."

"Okay." Christie reached for Wes's hand.

"I'm your aunt," Ruby Hart continued. "After my twin sister married your father, he hired me to come work for him as his lab assistant. While she was pregnant with you, she was exposed to one of the deadly viruses manufactured by a group of rogue scientists. Technically, all three of us were — me, your dad, and my sister — though she seemed to have gotten the worst of it. Your dad and I had been working late, and your mother had brought us dinner. It's unclear if the exposure was an accident or something more sinister. It all happened so quickly. Long story short, your father swiped several vials of the vaccine. Sadly, my sister died within hours of receiving it. Though you were delivered prematurely, you survived."

By now, Christie was gripping his hand very tightly.

Dan gave a long, low whistle.

"There are no official records of anything that happened

that night," Mrs. Hart concluded. "Your father made sure of it. Since my sister and I happened to come from a live-off-the-grid kind of family, it made our subsequent switcharoo all the easier to pull off. There were no pesky medical records out there for anyone to check or challenge."

"Let me guess." Dan whistled again. "His lab assistant tragically perished in a work-related accident that night." He put air quotes around the words *lab assistant*. "Then the grieving aunt returned home masquerading as Jimmy Hart's wife to help him protect his trillion-dollar baby from the rogue scientists."

Ruby Hart nodded grimly. "That about sums it up."

Christie stared wide-eyed at her aunt. "Did you love my dad?" she quavered.

"Very much, sweetheart." Her aunt's expression softened. "How could I not? He was the kindest, most brilliant man I've ever met. Not to mention the handsomest."

"I appreciate you telling me the truth." Looking dazed, Christie stood and walked around the table to hug Ruby Hart from behind. "You'll always be my mother, though. Please assure me you're not trying to weasel out of that."

"Never!" Ruby fondly patted the hands Christie had clasped around her shoulders.

"Good." Christie's eyes were damp as she leaned down to kiss her aunt's cheek. "Because I wasn't planning on letting you weasel out of anything." She kept her arms wrapped around the only mom she'd ever known while Dan informed them of the real reason he'd been sent to town.

"I don't know what renewed those rogues' interest in you and your aunt after all this time, Christie. All I can assure you of is this. I want to bring these scoundrels to their knees as badly as you do, along with the law firm currently representing them."

"His family's firm," Bonnie supplied tightly. "I wasn't at

liberty to say that upstairs while the recording devices were on, but they're essentially holding our son hostage to buy our cooperation."

"Cooperation for what, exactly?" Wes narrowed his gaze at his sister.

"Right now, our orders are to get close to you and report back everything we see and hear that might lead to the files Jimmy Hart allegedly stole."

"This is all my fault." Mrs. Hart waved a hand weakly in the air. "I knew I was being watched, but I got careless the night I was researching the jewelry firm who made your dad's ring drive."

"A ring drive?" Dan gave a bark of laughter. "So that's how Mr. Hart made it out of the lab with the files in question?"

Mrs. Hart nodded ruefully.

"That's genius!"

"It's been missing ever since his death," she sighed. "So I'm not sure how genius it was after all."

"It's actually not, er, missing." Christie dropped her arms from around her aunt.

Ruby Hart slowly tipped her face up to meet the gaze of her niece. "You lied to me?" she gasped. "All this time, you've been lying to me?"

"It was more a matter of omission." Christie bit her lower lip. "Like you pointed out on more than one occasion, I never outright denied having it in my possession."

"That doesn't make it right," Mrs. Hart protested, looking aghast.

Christie raised and lowered her shoulders. "It was the last thing Dad gave me before he died. It was like having a piece of him with me all these years. In my defense, I didn't know about the memory drive hidden on it until a few days ago."

Her aunt continued looking horrified. "How did you keep it from every last scallywag who came searching for it?"

Christie shrugged again. "Honestly? I wasn't aware anyone was looking for it."

"Did you keep it in a safe or a lockbox or...?"

Christie snickered. "Let's see. It's been inside a stack of chip bowls in the kitchen, down inside the toes of various boots, sometimes in the pocket of my jeans while I was riding Prancer, and the list goes on."

Her mother made a rueful sound. "You mean it's been hiding in plain sight all this time?"

"I guess you could call it that." Christie waved a hand. "I knew you would only search in the most obvious places, so it really wasn't too difficult."

"Where is it?" Her aunt half-rose from her chair.

Wes looked questioningly at Christie, and she nodded. He removed the ring drive from his pocket and slid it across the table to Ruby Hart.

She lifted it in awe. "The last thing your father said to me, Christie, was that he gave you something that would eventually make everything right again. He didn't get the chance to explain what he meant, but I got the impression he was referring to the law degree he expected you to hold someday."

As Christie's lips parted to speak, Ruby raised her head to meet her niece's gaze. "Don't you dare apologize! You became what you were meant to become."

Wes appreciated her laying that demon to rest. He'd gotten the impression on more than one occasion that it was something that had been gnawing at Christie over the years.

A lull crept into the conversation.

"Well," Bonnie broke in softly, "we happen to have a lot of expertise sitting around this table — an attorney, two law students, a former police detective, and a former employee of the same pharmaceutical firm where Dr. Hart worked. It seems to me that the chips are a little stacked in our favor at the moment. Wouldn't you agree?"

Her question elicited a round of nods.

"Good." She folded her hands. "Then I suggest we buy a little time from those who think they're pulling Dan and my strings at the moment."

"How?" Ruby Hart looked fearful.

Dan covered his wife's hand, gently squeezing her fingers. "Feed them a few tidbits of information here and there, nothing serious. Just enough to whet their appetites for more. In the meantime, we'll examine every inch of the documents on that ring drive for anything we can use to bring these cockroaches to justice."

IN THE END, THEY AGREED TO USE WES'S COMPUTER, because it was set up with the most safeguards against hackers. Within the hour, he'd removed it from his office and carted it down the stairs to Christie's safe room. He went to work with Dan and Ruby peering over his shoulder. Christie and Bonnie made coffee for everyone and kept them supplied with snacks.

"There." Not too many minutes into their search, Christie's aunt pointed to a folder that Wes hadn't opened yet. It was labeled *Markers*.

Though he was unsure what he was looking at, he did as she requested. They found themselves staring at a series of blood test results — years' worth of them if Wes was reading them right.

Mrs. Hart gasped, looking faint. Then her eyes slowly filled with tears.

Wes stood and motioned for her to take a seat before she collapsed.

She gratefully sat. With a shaking hand, she pointed at the screen and explained what they were looking at.

"This is my sister's blood test an hour after Jimmy administered the vaccine to her. As you can see, there was no improvement in her condition. His conclusion in the days that followed was that he'd inadvertently administered a placebo to her. She never stood a chance," she choked.

Wes laid a hand on her shoulder. "I'm sorry."

She reached up and covered his hand with hers. "The emergency C-section saved Christie's life. By some miracle, she did not contract the virus in utero." She pointed at the computer screen again. "Jimmy and I were the only ones who actually received the vaccine. Here are his test results in the months that followed." She frowned at the screen. "According to his notes, he continued to carry a dormant form of the virus that eventually flared up again...and finally took his life." She fell silent again for a moment. "In the end, I'm the only one the vaccine worked on."

More tears flowed down her cheeks. "I always assumed he insisted on the body swap to protect Christie, but it looks like he did it to protect me from those rogues!"

Wes had watched enough sci-fi movies to imagine her being whisked away to some shadowy lab for endless experimentation in order to harvest the antibodies in her blood. There was no way he was going to let that happen, though.

Christie and Bonnie joined them at the computer while they grimly plowed through the rest of the contents of the *Markers* folder.

"The placebo is what made Jimmy suspicious," Mrs. Hart mused as she read through his journal entries and interpreted the scientific equations for the rest of them. "Otherwise, they might've truly gotten away with murder. He was building a case against them. One that accused them of performing unauthorized clinical trials on him, his pregnant wife, and me. They may still get away with it," she finished sadly, "since he was never able to identify who was behind this. According to his notes, they always wore masks when they visited the lab and addressed each other by code names."

"I think I can help with that," Dan announced quietly. "Since Evermore & Sons is representing the pharmaceutical firm, I happen to be in possession of a list of names, showing exactly who's behind this."

Mrs. Hart leaned weakly back in her chair. "Are you saying we finally have enough evidence to take to the police?"

"And then some," Wes assured in a voice rough with emotion.

Christie slid her arms around him, hugging him tightly. "Bet you never expected to close one of the biggest cases of the century after laying down your badge, huh?"

"You said it." He hugged her back, inwardly sending up a prayer of thanksgiving that she and her aunt were finally going to get the justice they deserved.

CHAPTER 11: HER BIGGEST PERFORMANCE

CHRISTIE

I t felt like the town itself had been holding its breath in excitement for this day to come. Posters advertising today's special production of Castellano's indoor rodeo were hanging in nearly every store window for three simple reasons: It was exactly one week before Christmas, it would be the last indoor rodeo of the year, and every employee would be dressed in holiday festive gear — even the horses. Since it was the town's first-ever holiday indoor rodeo, nobody wanted to miss it.

In true Pinetop fashion, snow was swirling against Christie's bedroom window when she awoke the morning of the show. It had been nice sleeping in her own bed again for the first time in weeks. The new bedroom suit she'd ordered online had finally arrived yesterday. Both Wes and Dan had helped her assemble it in the spare bedroom where her mother was now staying. She'd extended her visit indefinitely, even making noises about doing a little house shopping in town for herself soon.

As she brushed her teeth and tugged a filmy red sweater over her head, butterflies swarmed through her stomach like a whole flock of birds preparing to fly south for the winter. Today was a very big day, quite possibly the most challenging performance of her career.

She'd spent hours behind closed doors yesterday being briefed by Sheriff Dean Skelton and a bazillion other men and women in uniform. Wes claimed they were FBI, along with a few Homeland Security representatives, but he might've been pulling her leg.

Her mother met her at the bottom of the stairs, looking fabulous as usual in a long red corduroy dress. Her impossibly tiny waist was cinched in with a brown leather belt that matched her high-heeled western boots, and her platinum blonde hair was draped in a single loose braid over one shoulder.

Her gaze anxiously raked over her daughter. "Are you sure about—"

"Yes," Christie interrupted firmly. They'd been over this at least a dozen times already. "You're not the only one capable of making sacrifices for the people you love, Mom. It's my turn to take one for the team today."

The angles of Ruby Hart's high cheekbones seemed to soften. "Of all the things in this world I've had a hand in, you're the one thing I did right."

"We're in this together, Mom." Christie held out a fist.

Her mother bumped fists with her. "After this is over, we should both retire and take up something safe, like knitting."

"Absolutely not!" Christie gave her a mock glare. "We're not starting a cooking show together, either. It has to be something we're both good at."

"Like arguing?" her mother taunted.

They stared at each other a moment before dissolving into laughter.

"Speaking of arguing, you could both attend law school together," Wes suggested, striding across the living room.

Christie glanced over at him in surprise and delight. "I didn't know you were here!" She hadn't heard his arrival.

As he removed his Stetson and tossed it on the hall tree, her mother made herself scarce.

"You're early." She hadn't eaten breakfast yet and wondered if he had. If not, he could join her.

"Am I?" He reached for her hand, leaving her on the bottom step as he twined their fingers together. Because of the added inches she was standing on, they were at eye level.

"It's seven-thirty in the morning," she pointed out breathlessly. "You said you would be here at eight." She drank in the sight of his dark wavy hair and rugged good looks, tracing his firm jaw line with her eyes.

"Like what you see?" he asked huskily.

"I love it." She locked gazes with him. "And you."

He grew still. "What did you say?"

"I love you." She loved his steadiness and dependability, his strength and his enormous heart. Right now, she was also wildly grateful for his loyalty. Despite all the dangers plaguing her life since the moment they'd met, he'd remained faithfully by her side.

His dark eyes glinted with emotion as he relinquished her fingers to gently cradle her face between his hands. "I love you, too. Before we re-met and started dating, I didn't realize it was possible to feel this way about another person."

"Me, either," she murmured dreamily.

"I can no longer imagine any version of my future without you in it," he continued, gazing at her with such longing that it made her toes curl in her boots. "So, after the dust settles on today's sting operation, I hope you'll consider one more adventure." He leaned in to gently brush his mouth against hers. "Becoming a mechanic's wife."

"Wow!" she murmured against his lips. "We're going straight from the L word to the M word."

"You're not running and screaming," he pointed out, kissing her again.

"You do realize I may never master the art of cooking," she warned with a gurgle of laughter.

"Don't care." He ran a thumb across her lower lip, something he never seemed to grow tired of doing.

"And I may fluff up a few pounds now and then after binging on jelly donuts."

"Whatever," he scoffed. "I say we order a whole dozen of them this evening, indulge ourselves, then walk them off together."

"You mean skip dinner and go straight to dessert?"

"Yep."

She beamed a happy smile at him. "I really, really love you."

"So, is that a yes?"

"Wes!" Her eyes widened. "Are you seriously asking me to...?" She gulped, unable to finish the question.

"I am. Will you marry me, Christie?"

Her heart raced like a thousand horses on a stampede. "Yes."

With a whoop of exultation, he threw his arms around her and swept her off the stair, swinging her around and around in the entry foyer.

Her mother flew across the living room. "What's happening?"

"She said yes!" Wes stopped twirling her to crush their mouths together.

Five hours later

Wᴇꜱ ᴡᴀᴛᴄʜᴇᴅ ꜰʀᴏᴍ ᴛʜᴇ ᴇᴅɢᴇ ᴏꜰ ᴛʜᴇ ʀɪɴɢ ᴀꜱ ᴠᴀʀɪᴏᴜꜱ undercover law enforcement officials swept the room in Castellano's security guard uniforms, making last-minute adjustments to the cameras. They'd done a thorough job of setting them up. There were very few inches of real estate across the amphitheater where the cameras couldn't reach.

Though Wes's resignation from the police department had been officially signed off on, he was unofficially back on duty today — by choice and without pay. It was for a good cause. His fiancée needed his protection, and she would be the most vulnerable today during her trick riding performance. He was in a paramedic uniform, embedded with the medical evacuation team in order to remain right up there at the edge of the ring. He didn't plan to let her out of his sight after her performance began.

Angel Castellano stepped into the room to confer with two maintenance guys. As they strode closer, Wes ducked his head over his medical bag and pretended to be packing something back into place.

The maintenance guys stopped directly in front of him to point out something about the wiring that they weren't too thrilled about.

"Fix it," Angel said firmly. "I don't care about the cost. The safety of my staff and our guests comes first."

They nodded and took off to handle whatever it was.

Angel remained standing there with his back to Wes. "Are you ready for this?"

"Yep." Wes pretended to drop a roll of gauze. As it rolled to Angel's feet, he used it as an excuse to leap over the railing to retrieve it. When he straightened with it in his hand, he held out his hand for the benefit of anyone who was watching.

Angel shook it, scanning his features. He was in his usual

black trousers and white button-up shirt with the sleeves rolled to his elbows. His blazer was missing.

"Is there somewhere we can talk?" Wes tossed the roll of gauze in the air and caught it. Then he turned away to tuck it back in his medical bag.

"Dressing room four." Angel turned on his heel and strode away.

Wes waited until he was out of sight. Then he nonchalantly picked up his medical bag and made his way downstairs to the lower-level dressing rooms, whistling as if he didn't have a care in the world. After ensuring he wasn't being followed, he quickly let himself inside dressing room four.

Angel was waiting for him there. He wasn't alone. The dressing room had been turned into a security hub. Video monitors lined the walls, rolling live feeds of nearly every section of the amphitheater.

Four men with headsets were hunkered behind computers, watching the feeds. Only one of them looked up and nodded when he walked in.

He nodded back, recognizing one of the FBI field agents he'd met yesterday. "Nice set-up."

"No kidding! This is state-of-the-art facial recognition software, my friend." Angel peered in fascination at one of the live video feeds.

"Any action yet from the perps?"

For an answer, Angel aimed a remote control at one of the monitors on the wall and mashed a button. The faces of five middle-aged men and one older guy flashed across the screen in a photo montage. The older one was the rabid "fan" who'd been trailing Christie across town. Four of them Wes didn't recognize. The sixth one, however, made his insides tighten. It was one of the other paramedics pulling duty with him this afternoon.

Angel quietly explained how each of the men on the

screen had been flagged by his security team in recent days for trying to get too close to Christie before or after her performances.

"I married a celebrity country western singer," Angel concluded, "so this isn't my first brush with danger, but I've never seen this many creeps converging and colluding at the same time like this."

Neither had Wes. He was enormously grateful to have federal agents with boots on the ground working alongside Sheriff Skelton and his crew for today's sting operation.

In preparation, they'd spread a rumor and laid it on thick with the locals that Christie Hart was being scouted by a huge rodeo company. All across town, folks were whispering behind their hands. *If there's any truth to it, this could be her last performance in Pinetop.*

What the police were hoping to incite was a snatch and grab attempt that would bring most or all of the rogue pharmaceutical investors crawling out of the woodwork at the same time.

Angel turned on a laser beam pointer and aimed it at the scraggly super fan. "He's a billionaire investor in everything from AI butlers to holiday flavors of eggnog."

"After this afternoon, he's going to wish he stuck with eggnog," Wes promised darkly.

Rodeo time

ROMAN STUCK TO CHRISTIE LIKE A COCKLEBUR THE ENTIRE time she was getting Prancer into his Christmas gear — red socks, a green saddle blanket, plus red and white striped reins. Christie was in a solid red body suit made of fabric that glimmered like crystal. It had fringed sleeves and fringe running down the outside of each leg.

Roman even walked her to the edge of the arena.

"Is everything okay?" She didn't mind the company, but because of the enhanced security this evening, she already had plenty of folks hovering over her.

He bent his head closer to hers. "Caught a new ranch hand loitering around Prancer's stall earlier. Though I sent him on his way, I thought you should be aware."

"Thanks, Roman." She wished she could tell him that the guy had been FBI, but it wasn't her place. The Castellano's staff members had been briefed on a need-to-know basis only, and Roman hadn't been deemed as someone who needed to know. She envied him his ignorance and sorta wished they could trade places right now.

"You betcha." He cupped his hands to give her a boost up.

As she took her place in the saddle, Roman stepped back to lean against the railing. He propped a boot on the lowest rung.

As she rode Prancer closer to the starting gate, Wes's voice sounded over the earpiece tucked inside her right ear. "Looks like my competition is trying to get a leg up on me."

"Very funny." She smiled at his pun.

"I have my moments."

She drew a deep breath to brace herself for what was coming as she glanced around the festive amphitheater. Pre-lit garlands were wrapping the railing around the entire riding ring. Every few feet, they were punctuated by a red velvet bow. The ceiling was alight with upside down Christmas trees drenched in tinsel and bright ornament balls.

"Want to hear my favorite scripture?" Wes inquired softly. "My partner and I used to quote it to each other when we knew we were heading into a tough situation."

"Yes, please."

"The Lord Himself goes before you and will be with you; He will never leave you nor forsake you. Do not be afraid; do not be discouraged."

It was the perfect verse and exactly what she'd needed to hear. "Thank you, Wes."

"I love you, Christie."

"I love you, too." She eyed the packed stands. It looked like a record crowd. People of all ages were present, whole families with children. Most people were dressed in holiday colors — everything from ugly sweaters to reindeer headbands to light-up necklaces. It made Christie glad all over again that she'd chosen such a fun and cheerful small town to live and work in. Pinetop was like a well-kept secret. The rumor about her being scouted away by a bigger rodeo firm couldn't have been further from the truth. No amount of money would be taking her away from their super hunky mechanic shop owner, whom she had every intention of marrying soon.

A rodeo queen dressed as Mrs. Santa rode into the center of the arena, waving the Arizona flag to start the show. Then Angel and Willa Castellano gave a short, heartfelt presentation that included a hint that a very important special guest might be making an appearance this evening.

The children started cheering loudly and chanting, "Santa! Santa! Santa!"

Then it was Christie's turn. She rode into the ring with her knees pulled up against her chest, feet in the saddle.

The audience was clapping and shouting before she stood and started to wave. Most of them had seen her perform before, so they knew this was how she began each show.

She rode one full lap around the ring, holding her candy cane striped reins in one hand and waving with the other hand. On her second lap, she dropped the reins and waved with both hands.

Immediately afterward, she dropped into a shoulder stand, and the cheer grew louder. Before she could right herself, there was a collective gasp across the room.

Unsure of what they were reacting to, she continued her routine, doing a spinning flip to seat herself backwards on Prancer. That was when she realized she was no longer alone in the ring. Another pair of horses were galloping in pursuit of her. Both riders were dressed like Christmas elves, and both were twirling lassos.

This isn't part of the show. Her heart pounded at the realization that these were the men who'd been paid to abduct her. Apparently, they had no idea how many law enforcement officials were on deck in the theater today.

It'll be your funeral.

The first lasso zinged in her direction, narrowly missing her as she ducked. The audience laughed and cheered her on as she dodged the second lasso. When one of the elves playfully shook his fist in the air, the audience booed him.

"Hang on, babe. We've got five of them in our crosshairs." Wes's voice sounded across her earpiece again. "Just waiting on one more thug to show his ugly head." Though he was trying to be soothing, she could hear the edge of concern in his voice.

A clown car zipped into the ring. She wasn't sure if it was being driven by friends or foes. During her brief moment of distraction, one of the elves' lassoes settled over her shoulders, tightening like a vise.

"Wes?" she called in agitation.

He didn't answer.

The two galloping horses converged on either side of her. With her arms imprisoned, she was powerless to defend herself when she was tugged belly down onto the horse to her right.

With a whinny of alarm, Prancer cantered alone toward

the exit gate. The clown car led the way, zipping across the ring in front of the horses. When they reached the exit gate, hands tugged her to the ground where she was transferred to the clown car.

Panic filled Christie's throat at the fear that something must have gone terribly awry with the FBI's plan. Where were they? She was being abducted in front of hundreds of people who were doing nothing to help her, since they assumed it was part of the show. And why wouldn't they? Angel and Willa had promised them a special guest appearance.

A prayer bubbled to her lips. "Please, God, don't let them take me out of this ring." If they succeeded, she might never see Wes, her mother, or her dearest friends again.

The lights in the auditorium suddenly flashed off, leaving nothing but the glimmering garlands on the railings.

Dark shadowy creatures leaped into the arena, surrounding Christie and her captors. It was over before she could hardly blink. No more than half a minute passed before the lights flipped back on, flooding the room once again.

She found herself clutched in Santa's arms. No, not Santa. It was Wes, with a Santa costume thrown haphazardly over his paramedic uniform. With a shriek of relief, she threw her arms around his neck.

He cuddled her close. "I've got you, babe."

The audience broke into deafening cheers and applause, assuming he'd rescued her from the naughty elves.

"It took you long enough," she grumbled in his ear.

"I'll explain everything the moment we're backstage. You've got some smiling and waving to do first, though, since you're the star of the show."

She waved a shaky hand at the audience, and their cheers grew louder.

"What do you think they'd do if Santa kissed you right now?" he teased in her ear.

Her face grew warm. She imagined it was as red as the outfits they were both wearing. "Just promise me one thing, Wes."

"Anything, babe."

"Is it finally over?"

"Not at all." He grinned and twirled her in a full circle to the delight of their audience. "I'm pretty sure our next chapter is just beginning."

EPILOGUE

Christmas Eve

"Thank you, Mom." Christie gazed down at the lovely white velvet column dress that hugged her figure and draped all the way to the floor. She had no idea how her mother had gotten her hands on such a gorgeous dress at the last minute like this. After twenty-seven years, however, she was finally learning not to question Ruby Hart. There was seriously nothing the woman wouldn't do for the few people in the world she loved. And the man who was about to become her son-in-law was one of those people.

"You're welcome, hon." Her mother reached out to smooth a hand over the fabric against her shoulder and tweak the pearl necklace resting against her throat. The necklace had once belonged to Jimmy Hart's mother. Christie was thrilled to be wearing it on her wedding day. Though her mother still was — and always would be — a hoarder, she'd finally passed down a few mementoes, to include a porcelain dog paperweight Christie had always coveted from her father's desk.

"You look pretty nice yourself." She eyed her mother's emerald green jumpsuit and silver pumps.

Her mother merely shrugged. She was accustomed to turning heads.

"I asked Roman to help me keep an eye on you today," Christie continued solemnly.

"What now?" her mother sighed.

"Pretty sure one of those FBI agents was checking you out the other day." He'd remained in town, too, claiming he was helping the local police department wrap up the paperwork on the case.

"Oh." Her mother snorted. "I thought you were serious."

"What if I am?"

Ruby Hart's gaze took on a faraway look. "Your father was the love of my life, hon." She drew a tremulous breath. "Gosh, but he would've given anything to see you like this on your wedding day!"

Christie blinked back sad-happy tears.

Fortunately for her makeup, Bonnie chose that moment to dance across the room and join them in front of the long dressing mirror in Willa Castellano's office. "You're the most beautiful bride in the world," she gushed, "isn't she, Dannie?" Stooping down to hug her son, she pointed up at Christie. "Tell your Aunt Christie that she's pretty. Pret-ty," she repeated slowly.

"Pitty," he repeated, testing out the word.

At his mother's gurgle of laughter, he repeated it more loudly, clapping his hands. "Pitty! Pitty! Pitty!" He was serving as their ring bearer today, in a tiny gray suit with a white rose boutonniere pinned to his lapel. He'd already pulled it off twice, so the outer petals were hanging a little limp.

"Yes, she is, you handsome little fella!" Her mother held out a hand and coaxed Dan Junior to give her a high five.

Ever since the roundup had begun of the rogue pharmaceutical investors, Evermore & Sons had been under constant attack by the press for their willingness to provide legal representation to such a heinous criminal enterprise. Corporate clients were pulling their accounts from them right and left. The stock price of the pharmaceutical company had additionally plummeted overnight. Dan's dad was so busy putting out fires that he'd all but tossed Dan Junior back in Dan's arms when he'd flown to San Francisco to pick him up. Neither he nor Bonnie expected the Evermores to cause them any more heartache for the foreseeable future — certainly not while they were being tried so harshly in the court of public opinion.

A text message buzzed across Bonnie's phone screen. "It's time, ladies and gents." She beamed a happy smile at Ruby Hart. "You first, Mom."

Nodding, Mrs. Hart took her place at the door of the office. In moments, Angel Castellano appeared.

Though Christie's boss wasn't nearly old enough to be her father, he'd agreed to walk both her and her mother down the aisle today. Or across the theater, in their case, since Christie and Wes were getting married at his dinner theater.

Dan appeared at the door next to escort Bonnie and Dan Junior down the aisle. Bonnie had warned Christie that the only way Dannie would make it through the ceremony was if his little hand remained in hers.

Angel reappeared in the doorway. "Your turn, Christie." He was in one of his signature black suits, this time with the jacket on and a tie knotted over his dress shirt.

"I really appreciate your doing this," she breathed, taking his arm.

"I'm truly honored." He crinkled his eyes at her. "You've really put Castellano's on the map the last few months."

"I'm pretty sure you were already on the map, Angel." He had a hand in at least a dozen charities across town. Plus, he employed a significant number of the locals. However, she knew what he was trying to say.

"True, but you've helped take us to the next level, and for that, my wife and I are grateful." He escorted her down the hallway leading away from the administrative offices to the main theater.

"I'm glad." She smiled up at him. "It was super fun getting in on the ground floor of your indoor rodeo." She'd made so many friends. And somewhere along the way, Pinetop had become her home. "In fact, there's nowhere else I'd rather be. I hope you were planning on keeping a trick rider around for a while."

"I most definitely am." He grinned down at her. "I know it was only part of the build-up for our sting operation, but that rumor about you being scouted away really rankled with the staff at Castellano's. Nobody here is ready to give you up."

"Thank you." She squeezed his arm gratefully as the opening notes of the wedding march were played. "Oh, wow!" she whispered, as he led her into the theater.

The stage had been reassembled in the center of the room, and a forest of Christmas trees had been set in place. They twinkled with thousands of tiny white lights, forming a brilliant background for the oversized white rose trellis at the base of the stage.

Wes Wakefield waited for her beneath it, his tall frame nearly filling it.

She sashayed in his direction, hardly able to believe they would be married by Christmas. Her head was still spinning over how quickly he'd pushed through their marriage license at City Hall. It probably helped that he had gazillions of friends in law enforcement and governmental positions.

They reached the rose trellis, and Angel transferred her hand from his arm to Wes's arm. "God bless you both," he said warmly. Then he stepped back to join his wife, who was standing beside Christie's mother in the front row. No less than three rows of Wes's policemen buddies were standing behind them.

As she and Wes faced the minister together, Wes whispered huskily, "I love you, Christie!"

She mouthed the words, "I love you," back to him. Then the ceremony began. It was woven with scriptures of love and verses to commemorate the birth of their Lord and Savior. After they exchanged their vows, the minister ended the ceremony with one of Christie's all-time favorite verses.

"*Glory to God in the highest, and on earth peace, good will toward men*. By the powers vested in me by God and the State of Arizona, I pronounce you husband and wife. You may kiss the bride."

Wes gently brushed his mouth over hers. "You're the best Christmas gift ever, Mrs. Wakefield."

She touched his cheek, very happy with her end of the deal — her cowboy mechanic, husband, and best friend. Always and forever.

Starting right now.

Ready to read about wrangler Roman Rios's not-a-date with just-a-friend that accidentally turns into a little bit more?
Keep turning for a peek at
Cowboy On-the-Job Boyfriend for Christmas
a sweet, slow-burn Christmas workplace romance!

SNEAK PREVIEW: COWBOY ON-THE-JOB BOYFRIEND FOR CHRISTMAS

No *more workplace romance for her!*

A rising star at a small-town dinner theater, Hope Isaacson has big plans for the future. Plans that don't involve dating on the job. She tried that once, and it ended in disaster. But when a good friend and coworker begs her to serve as his plus one at a family holiday celebration, she decides to make an exception. Just this once.

After being tragically widowed, Roman Rios has no interest in dating again. So a one-time date with his just-a-friend coworker feels like the perfect way to get his matchmaking sister off his back. One excuse leads to another, and their fake relationship extends to a second date and a third.

Both of them are suddenly dying to know where their unexpected attraction might lead...

Hope you enjoyed this quick peek at
Cowboy On-the-Job Boyfriend for Christmas

This series is available in eBook, paperback, and Kindle Unlimited on Amazon!

A VERY COUNTRY CHRISTMAS WISH
Read them all!
Cowboy Angel in Disguise for Christmas
Cowboy Foreman in Love for Christmas
Cowboy Blind Date Mix-Up for Christmas
Cowboy On-the-Job Boyfriend for Christmas
Cowboy Single Dad Crush for Christmas
Cowboy Grumpy Boss for Christmas
Cowboy Friend Zone for Christmas
Cowboy Stolen Kiss for Christmas
Cowboy Accidentally Hitched for Christmas

GET A FREE BOOK!

Join my mailing list to be the first to know about new releases, free books, special discount prices, Bonus Content, and giveaways.

https://BookHip.com/JNNHTK

NOTE FROM JO

Guess what? I have some Bonus Content for you. Read more about the swoony cowboy heroes in my books (more first kisses, more weddings, more babies...) by signing up for my mailing list.

There will be a special Bonus Content chapter for each new book I write, exclusively for my subscribers. Plus, you get a FREE book just for signing up!

Thank you for reading and loving my books.

JOIN CUPPA JO READERS!

If you're on Facebook, you're invited to join my group, Cuppa Jo Readers. Saddle up for some fun reader games and giveaways + book chats about my sweet and swoony cowboy book heroes!

https://www.facebook.com/groups/CuppaJoReaders

SNEAK PREVIEW: OPPOSITES ATTRACT HERO

A *big-city police detective butts heads with a small-town realtor over the best way to catch a criminal in this sweet, opposites-attract romance.*

Detective Zayden Wolfe is tall. Award-winning realtor Alice Underwood is short. He's serious; she's hilarious, especially when she's nervous or on edge — which is where he's been keeping her since the moment they met.

Oh, and she's totally not buying his claim about transferring from the Dallas Police Department to the country, simply to enjoy the farm-fresh air. He's up to something, and she'd happily expose whatever it is if she wasn't so busy trying to stop a ruthless band of criminal land developers.

Turns out he's after the same thugs, which are now after her, forcing the two of them to work together and finally deal with the spark of attraction they've been fighting.

Grab your copy of Opposites Attract Hero and binge through this sweet, small-town romantic suspense series today!

Opposites Attract Hero.
Available in eBook, paperback, hard cover large print, and Kindle Unlimited!

Read them all!
A - Accidental Hero
B - Best Friend Hero
C - Celebrity Hero
D - Damaged Hero
E - Enemies to Hero
F - Forbidden Hero
G - Guardian Hero
H - Hunk and Hero
I - Instantly Her Hero
J - Jilted Hero
K - Kissable Hero
L - Long Distance Hero
M - Mistaken Hero
N - Not Good Enough Hero
O - Opposites Attract Hero

Much love,
Jo

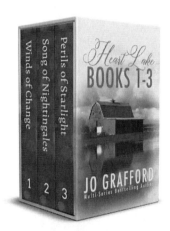

You get **THREE** *full-length novels featuring sweet cowboys, feel-good romance, and inspirational stories with a twist of suspense in this Heart Lake romance collection!*

Winds of Change: Getting hired as a high school principal in her hometown is a dream come true in this sweet, enemies-to-lovers romance, except for one small detail — her ex is the new head of security...

Song of Nightingales: A billionaire heartbreaker turning over a new leaf and the small town family doctor he falls for — the one woman he can't have in this opposites attract romance...

Perils of Starlight: A policeman who exclusively works the night shift to hide his scarred face, a lovely detective determined to solve a cold case, and the trail of clues that leads to an accidental attraction...

Grab your copy!
Heart Lake Box Set #1

HEART LAKE BOX SETS
Read them all!
Heart Lake Box Set #1 (books 1-3)
Heart Lake Box Set #2 (books 4-6)
Heart Lake Box Set #3 (books 7-9)

Much love,
Jo

SNEAK PREVIEW: THE BILLIONAIRE'S BIRTHDAY BLIND DATE

I *'m happy for you.*

Eloise Cantona stormed down the sidewalk as fast as the four-inch heels of her Gianvito Rossi mesh pumps would allow. She'd been repeating those words inside her head a bazillion times per day for the past two months, hoping she would finally start to believe them.

Of course she should be happy for her brother! Only a completely awful sister wouldn't be. Roman deserved every ounce of joy he'd found with Celine Petrova, his pop singing fiancee, and then some. The guy worked 24/7 running their family business. He deserved to love and be loved.

But so did Eloise; didn't she?

Yet here she was — the oldest of four siblings at the ripe age of twenty-nine — without so much as an engagement ring on her finger. It wasn't as if she had trouble finding boyfriends or keeping them. In fact, she was currently dating the smoking-hot vice president of a mega commercial construction firm. One with crazy beautiful beach-blonde hair and an Aussie accent that she could seriously listen to all day long. Most unfortunately, her Down Under date always seemed to be on some business trip or another and, well, her biological clock was ticking faster than ever. So he probably wasn't "the one."

Muffling a sigh of self pity, Eloise quickened her pace as a church bell gonged the noon hour. It served as a reminder that she was running late, as usual. *Story of my life.* Gals in stilettos moved slower than the rest of the world.

Thankfully, Thea Ferrell understood that high style came at a price. Thea was one of her dearest friends. She was also the prime time interior design show host that Eloise was supposed to meet at their favorite bay-front cafe fifteen minutes ago.

Wait up! I'm coming.

If it hadn't been for that last minute call about her order for the copper ceiling tiles, she would've already been there. She rounded the corner of the ivory high-rise that housed Cantona Enterprises, her family's hotel conglomerate. Despite her agitation, she couldn't help enjoying the view. It overlooked the sparkling blue water of the Corpus Christi Bay, which was dotted with boats this afternoon. Sailboats, fishing boats, houseboats, and yachts — all floating against the backdrop of the Harbor Bridge and the midday sun.

As she clacked her way down a set of concrete stairs to the Bayside Cork & Grill, a seagull squawked past her, making her duck and reach for the railing. Her unzipped briefcase slipped from her grasp and bounced, open side first, down the stairs. Several manilla folders slid free from their black leather pockets, and the papers from within fluttered in too many directions to keep track of.

Eloise watched in dismay as all three dozen pages of her two o'clock design presentation took flight on the breeze. *This so isn't turning out to be my day!* Reaching for her cell phone, Eloise tapped out a quick text to her executive assistant.

Need another copy of my 2:00 file printed. Don't ask!

"Whoa!" a familiar baritone chided. "I'm pretty sure text-walking is prohibited here on the bay front."

Elon? Eloise glanced up in surprise, mechanically pressing the send button on her phone. "Elon! What are you doing here?" She and Thea were close, but she and Elon Carnegie were closer. They'd grown up together, attended the same private schools, and been besties for as long as she could remember — a popular fact with zero of her boyfriends, the current one included.

"Looking for you, sugar." Sauntering up the stairs in her direction, he shot her one of his devastating half smiles that tended to make women swoon. Though they were just friends, her heart did a quick cartwheel to have all that slate gray-eyed intensity focused on her.

Although the average onlooker probably assumed they were a couple, Eloise knew the endearments he continually showered on her were only part of his southern charm. He'd been born and raised in Texas, the same as she had been, but his family had roots in the deep south. The very deep south, thanks to one set of grandparents in Atlanta and another set in the Louisiana bayou. You could practically smell the pecan pies and gumbo, as well as hear the wind in the magnolia trees every time he spoke.

Though she hated the thought of passing up a visit with him, Eloise couldn't afford to cancel her lunch date with Thea. They were hashing their way through the details of an upcoming showcase of Eloise's award-winning designs. It was a key part of the next quarter's marketing campaign.

Instead, she contented herself with watching as he stooped in his designer black pinstripe suit to retrieve her briefcase and the few folders and papers that hadn't yet blown away. He straightened to face her with a bemused smile.

"I would insist on the full story about last night's golf tourney, but I'm supposed to have lunch with Thea," she sighed with a regretful wave of her hand. She let him hold her briefcase a little longer than necessary to keep him talking. "A working lunch full of fabric swatches, paint colors, and tile samples. Not nearly as exciting as the trophy you took home from your charity match."

He was a really good golfer, one who probably could've made a career of it on the professional circuit. To the best of her knowledge, though, he'd only played in charity fundraisers and for the sheer enjoyment of it. He claimed he was too busy running his family's golf franchise, Carnegie Golf, to hit the greens any more often than he did. She supposed serving as their CEO was a halfway decent excuse.

He stepped to the stair directly below hers to bring them eye to eye. "I happen to find your adventures in hotel design entertaining." He mounted the final stair to stand beside her. Leaning over to brush a kiss against her cheek, he gave her a whiff of his signature aftershave.

The scent made her think of moonlight, ocean waves, and quiet evenings — three things she didn't get to enjoy nearly enough with her hectic design schedule.

Keeping her briefcase clasped at his side, Elon inquired, "How about I go ahead and escort you to that table Thea went to so much trouble to reserve for y'all?"

Sheesh! What's with all the guilt-tripping?

Eloise scowled at him, while managing to appreciate the way the coastal breeze was tousling his hair. It was a rich shade of brown that always made her think of dark Belgian chocolate. She resisted the urge to reach up and smooth back a wave that blew across his eyes. Once upon a time, their carefree friendship would have allowed for such a casual gesture, but a new tension had sprung between them in recent months that made her keep her hand at her side.

Instead, she reached for the handle of her briefcase, which he didn't immediately release. Their fingers brushed while holding it between them.

Eloise gave it a light tug, but he still didn't release it.

"Is that a no?" he taunted softly.

Eloise tasted a curious mixture of irritation and relief. "I take it Thea ditched me." Meaning her mad dash from her office, her near tumble down the stairs, and the subsequent loss of her paperwork had all been for nothing.

"Now, darling," he chided in a mild voice. "Everyone knows the early bird gets the worm, and you are far from early."

Ugh! She despised gooey, squishy worms, even the mention of them. "On the contrary, being fashionably late has its clear benefits." She lifted her chin. Being late to meetings and making dramatic entrances happened to be one of her biggest talents. Since she was usually sitting on the buyer's side of the table — as the lead interior designer for her family's company, she purchased a heck of a lot of paint, furnishings, and construction services — being late had the effect of making the seller edgy. More anxious to negotiate on prices and other terms.

"If you're referring to being late enough to snag lunch with your favorite southern gentleman," he arched his brows in a challenge, "then, yes. Being late has some very choice benefits."

Without waiting for her response, he finished twisting her briefcase from her grasp and splayed one large hand against her lower back. "After you, princess." He angled his head at the remaining few stairs.

Feeling a bit put out over the way Thea had abandoned their lunch engagement without so much as a text message, Eloise swept past him, pondering whether she owed the television show hostess an apology for her lateness.

The waiter took one look at the two of them and waved them past the long line of patrons waiting to be seated. "If you'll follow me, sir. Ma'am."

No longer enjoying the bay views, Eloise sat wordlessly in the chair Elon held out for her. She unrolled the white linen napkin from her silverware and gave it a vicious shake before placing it in her lap. "Did Thea look angry when she left?"

Maybe Eloise should have made a point of arriving early instead of late for this particular appointment. Maybe she should have skipped that last phone call and missed the chance to cut a deal on the price of those copper tiles. Cantona Enterprises was counting on the prime time feature she'd been negotiating with Thea for months. The new marketing campaign was key to the grand opening of their newest resort on Crystal Beach.

"She didn't look angry to me."

It was a table for two in the farthest corner of the cafe. To their right was the railing overlooking the water. Pulling out the seat across from her, Elon folded his tall, rangy frame comfortably in it and fixed her with another one of his lazy smiles. "In fact, she looked pretty grateful when I picked up the tab for her lunch and had it packaged to-go."

"What?" Eloise gaped at him. "You mean you purposefully cancelled my lunch date with Thea?"

"I did," he assured, not looking the least repentant for his sins. "She told me to give you her love as well as her promise to reschedule. Then she dashed off to get ready for her next air time." He reached for Eloise's hand. "See? No harm done."

She shook his hand off. "I need that show."

"I know that, and Thea knows that." He reached inside the pocket of his suit jacket and produced a hastily scrawled note from Thea. Waving it at her between two fingers, he announced, "She said you can have the first pick of any of these dates and times."

Eloise reached greedily for the precious slip of paper, but he held it out of reach. "Lunch first. Then business."

"Elon!" she gasped. "What are you doing?" She couldn't remember him ever — in all their many years of friendship — being so high-handed with her professional affairs. He was dangerously close to crossing a line.

"Trying very hard to steal a lunch date with my best friend," he retorted in the same smooth voice. Pocketing the slip of paper once more, he drawled, "You don't write. You don't call."

"I've been busy," she protested, feeling suddenly weary. No, not just busy — insanely busy. She'd been working seventy and eighty-hour weeks, meeting herself coming and going. Then again, Elon knew how hard she worked. Why make an issue of it today, all of a sudden?

"I work long hours, too, but I still find time to shoot you a text message now and then." He waved a warning finger at her. "You, on the other hand, haven't bothered to respond to my last three."

"You're right. I'm sorry." She briefly closed her eyes, feeling awash with guilt about the alarming number of unread messages piling up in her inbox from, well, everyone she cared about.

"And you turned me down flat when I offered to take you to dinner last Saturday."

She opened her eyelids on a groan. "Fen swore he was going to be in town, but..." Her complete sweetie pie of a boyfriend had gotten tied up with work, which happened all too often — not that she blamed him. Fenston Barclay's family ran a booming commercial construction business, which required him to travel four to five days per week.

"And the weekend before that?" Elon prodded, looking grave.

"Same reason." Her insides were starting to hurt. "Why

are we doing this, Elon? What do you want from me?" It was starting to feel like he was accusing her of something, which made no sense. They were friends — the very best of friends. Though her work schedule had caused her to neglect him a bit recently, she'd not broken any rules that she knew of.

He started to speak, but their waiter reappeared with a silver tray. Perched in the center of it were two frosty glasses of water with lemons hanging off the side. He served them with a flourish and straightened. "May I take your order?"

Since her stomach was in knots, Eloise shook her head. There was no way she could eat anything at this point.

Elon's slate gaze latched on to hers and held it steadily. "I'll have your Cedar Planked Salmon. She'd like your Lobster Tail platter. We'll share a dinner salad with raspberry vinaigrette. Oh, and we'd like two glasses of peach tea."

When her lips parted in shock, he shrugged. Watching their waiter walk away, he growled, "If this is going to be our last meal together, I want it to be a nice one."

"Our last—Elon! Seriously, what's going on? What's this really about?" His demeanor was starting to worry her. If they were a couple, which they weren't, she would have considered this to be a break-up.

"Well." He spread his hands, looking wry. "I think you've made it pretty clear that our lifetime of friendship is coming to an end."

Really? When did I do that?

"I would never do such a thing!" she spluttered, indignant at such an unfair accusation. So she'd missed a few text messages. *Big deal*. She'd already explained how busy she'd been lately. "Our friendship means everything to me." So much so, that the idea of losing him for good brought her close to tears.

She studied him through narrowed lids. Had he starting dating someone unbeknownst to her? Was this his way of saying there was no more room for her in his life because of his new relationship?

After a pause, Elon folded his arms. His normally empathetic expression was unreadable. "Prove it," he demanded coolly.

"Prove what?" she asked helplessly, half expecting him to break into a laugh and tell her this was all some sort of joke. He'd always been a bit of a prankster. She glanced around them at the crowded cafe. It was a popular lunchtime dive. The tables were jammed with patrons. Not an empty chair was in sight.

"That our friendship still means something to you," he stated in the same cool, succinct tone.

Okay, so you aren't joking.

"How?" She reached for her glass of tea to get rid of the sudden dryness in her throat.

"That's for you to figure out, sugar." A ghost of a smile tugged at his mouth, though it didn't reach his eyes. "I have a birthday coming up. How about you surprise me?"

Oh. My. Lands!

She'd completely forgotten about his birthday.

The way he was shaking his head at her told her that he'd already deduced that sorry fact for himself.

Before she could apologize or say anything in her defense, their food arrived. The lobster tails were smothered in the cafe's secret sauce and perched on an artistically arranged mountain of steamed cauliflower, carrots, and asparagus.

Elon reached for her hand again and said a quick word of grace over their meal. To her surprise, he toyed with her fingers afterward instead of letting them go.

"This looks amazing." She lifted her fork, mouth already watering.

"Yes."

She flicked another glance across the table to discover

him studying her as if he was seeking something. "Why are you looking at me like that?"

"Because you're even more beautiful than the last time I saw you."

A chuckle escaped her. It felt good to laugh after the tense moment they'd been sharing. "No, really."

"Really." He let go of her hand at last and dug into his salmon. Making a sound of appreciation, he winked at her. "Best salmon I've ever had."

Feeling a flush of appreciation warm her cheeks, she waved her fork at him to hide her confusion. "You said that the last time we ate here."

"No, I'm pretty sure I said if you stick a bite of it on top of my head, my tongue would beat my brains out trying to get to it."

She burst out laughing. He was like a walking almanac when it came to southern wisdom and humorous old sayings. "I've really missed this," she declared softly. "I've missed us." And she had. Elon had been right to call her out on the way she'd been neglecting their friendship.

He raised and lowered his shoulders. "Like I said, sugar, you can prove it on my birthday."

She shook her head at his persistence. "That's less than three weeks away." It didn't give her much time to perform miracles.

"I've never seen you run from a challenge, doll."

She made a face at him as another thought struck her. "Your birthday also happens to be the day after my brother's wedding." *Ugh!* That was bad timing. *Really* bad timing.

Elon looked unperturbed. "So? He'll be on his honeymoon by then, leaving you as free as a cricket in sunshine to deliver my birthday surprise."

She smiled at his words as she pictured Roman and Celine's wedding venue. They were tying the knot on a private island in Fiji, which was drenched in sunshine year-round. She wasn't sure about the presence of crickets, though. Birthday Island was a romantic getaway where Roman had been inspired to propose a few months earlier during his birthday festivities.

A birthday resort!

An idea formed and grew, making Eloise sit up straighter. Her mind raced over the possibilities. "I think I just came up with the perfect surprise!" she announced in an ah-ha voice.

Elon's grey eyes twinkled wickedly across the table at her. "Guess we'll find out," he lifted his wrist to glance at his white gold Rolex, "in two more weeks and four more days."

"Got it." She rolled her eyes at the completely unnecessary reminder that the clock was ticking. "I just need you to do one thing for me first to help me get the details right."

"Anything for you, doll."

The way he was looking at her made her really glad Fen was out of town. Fen had never been overly happy about her continued friendship with Elon after they started dating. He probably wasn't going to like the fact she was planning a birthday celebration for Elon, either.

Which reminded her that Fen hadn't yet given her a firm yes to her invitation to serve as her plus one. Twisting his arm into coming to a wedding he probably didn't have the time to attend was another item on her impressively long to-do list. She swallowed a sigh of resignation as she reached for her cell phone.

"Finally going to read and respond to my texts, eh?" Elon teased.

She chuckled despite her weariness and clicked a few buttons. *Not yet.* "Actually, I'm going to send you a survey."

"About?" He cocked his head with interest.

"You." She beamed at him. "The questions are designed to help me deliver you the perfect birthday experience." She'd copied them from the Birthday Island's website. "I hope you'll take a peek at them."

He reached for her hand again. "Anything that brings that kind of smile to your face, sweetie, is well worth my time."

ELON STARED DOWN AT ELOISE'S PERFECT FRENCH manicure, entranced by the way each delicate finger curled so trustingly around his. They'd always shared this brand of casual intimacy, something he never failed to find both humbling and awe-inspiring. It hadn't paused until Fenston Barclay had come into their lives.

When Eloise and Fenston first started dating a few months ago, Elon had despised him on principle. There was simply no way to like the man who was dating the one woman Elon wished he had the courage to ask out. But he'd held his peace, liking the new sparkle in Eloise's gorgeous green eyes.

And then he'd had to stand by quietly and watch that sparkle die like it always did with her boyfriends, due to the thousand and one missteps each of them inevitably made with her. Though he would never tell her that, he considered her dating failures to be mostly her fault, since she was always picking the wrong guy to date — i.e. not him. He was already bracing himself for her next break-up. Fenston Barclay was about to be history; he could feel it.

He wasn't looking forward to the tears that would flow afterward. Since he happened to be between girlfriends right now, fortunately his shoulder was very much available to cry on.

But they couldn't go on like this forever. If she kissed enough frogs, she was bound to finally discover a prince who would pop the question. And what they were sharing right now would be over. For good.

The overriding sensation that time was running out made Elon long for the right moment and the right words that would finally turn his lifelong friendship with Eloise into something more. Over the past two years, he'd fantasized his way through countless scenarios, but the timing never seemed to be right. Either he was dating some friend's daughter his family had recommended to him — which never worked out — or Eloise was flitting like a butterfly on to the next guy, which also never worked out. It was a vicious cycle, one he was tired of repeating.

In the end, however, fear was the biggest thing that always ended up preventing him from asking her on a date — even during those brief moments of opportunity. The fear of losing her for good.

It was kinda terrifying, since he couldn't imagine a life she wasn't in. And right now she was in it, even though she wasn't filling the exact role he wanted her to fill. After years of fighting inner battles, he'd decided he'd rather be her best friend until the end of time than not have her at all. And there lay the problem: The moment he asked her on a date, she had the option of saying no.

Something he wasn't willing to risk.

"Hey! Are you even listening?" Eloise lightly tugged at the fingers he'd been toying with.

He reluctantly let them go, wishing he had the right to raise them to his mouth and kiss them one by one. "What's the rush, sugar?"

She flipped her long, strawberry blonde hair over her shoulder. "I need both hands to send you that survey."

Right. He could already picture the list of questions she was going to ask to construct his birthday surprise — all tidily numbered and rowed the way she organized her paint and fabric samples. Although he planned to humor her, he would have much preferred a birthday kiss any day over answering a bunch of silly questions.

The thought made his gaze lock on her pink glossy lips, which were pursed in concentration. He'd kissed other girls and felt next to nothing, but not once had he dared to kiss Eloise. Just the thought of it, though, made his heart pound.

"There," she announced, waving her phone at him. "I just sent them. Check your inbox."

His gaze rested a moment on the curve of her neck where it disappeared beneath her lacy white blouse and pale blue blazer. Her classy femininity took his breath away every time they were together. Though she had a weakness for wearing insanely high heels that made him live in constant fear of her tripping, she was —hands down — the most stylish woman he'd ever met. Not even the British royalty could hold a candle to his Eloise.

"Your wish is my command, love." He obediently dug for his phone and turned it on. Because he had her on speed dial and starred as a VIP on his phone list, he received a special notification each time she contacted him. All he had to do was tap the notification on his screen, and it took him straight to her email.

The list of requests and questions that popped up made him raise his brows. "Seems to me like you already know the answer to most of these." He scanned them from top to bottom. *Yep.* Eloise knew him inside and out. Not much new here.

"True," she demurred, glancing away, "but there were a few questions I wasn't one hundred percent sure about. Tell you what, you can skip the easy ones and focus on the hard ones."

"The hard ones, eh?" He scanned the list again. *What am I missing, doll?* "And those would be?"

"The second one," she declared without pause. "If you had a few hours to do anything you wanted, what would you do?"

I'd kiss you silly. "Hmm..." His mouth quirked. It was probably best to keep that one to himself.

"And I definitely don't know everything on your bucket list." She shot him a mischievous smile. "Oh, and are there any secret celebrity crushes you've been hiding from me?"

"Not a celebrity one, that's for sure," he scoffed, refusing to look up. It was a dangerous conversation to be having with Eloise, while she was in one of her sly moods. Heaven forbid that something in his expression might give away his true feelings about her! As the lead designer for Cantona Enterprises, she spent a decent amount of time in contract negotiations, which made her a whiz at reading and interpreting body language.

"Aha!" She pounced on his words like a vibrant kitten. "So you *are* secretly crushing on someone?"

Oh, yeah! Probably should have dodged that question altogether.

Then he chuckled as a new possibility struck him. Maybe, just maybe, they could have a little fun with her questions. He would throw a hint or two in his answers about the way he felt about her, then sit back and see where it led.

"What's so funny?" she asked suspiciously.

"You." He flicked off his phone. "The way you seem to think you're going to dig through my deepest, darkest secrets with a few questions and miraculously figure me out." He winked at her. "Not that easy, sugar. I'm a very complex man."

"As if." She snorted. "Well, maybe to the rest of the world you are. To me, you're an open book."

"Oh, really?" He leaned across the table, enjoying the fact that it brought him closer to her animated features. Earlier in their conversation, she'd gotten all closed-up looking and morose over the mention of Fenston Barclay, but her sparkle was back. "I triple-dog dare you to name my secret crush."

"Well, ah..."

If you get it right, darling, I'm going to throw caution to the wind and kiss you right here and now.

"Omigosh!" Her lovely green eyes rounded. "It's Piper, isn't it?"

"Who?" He frowned in confusion.

"That gorgeous golfing sensation at the last, er..." She snapped her fingers as if trying to jog the name from her memory.

"Nada. I already admitted that my secret crush isn't a celebrity." His gaze narrowed on hers. "I think we've also pretty well established the fact that you have no idea who I'm crushing on." He took it a step further, just to watch her reaction. "Who I've been crushing on for years..."

Eloise blinked in astonishment. Then a troubled look crept across her fine-boned features. "This sounds serious."

"It *is* serious," he assured in a low voice, hating the way his announcement had dimmed some of her sparkle again. "Then again, maybe it doesn't make sense to make that kind of change in my life. I'm all kinds of cool with remaining a single guy." *We don't have to go there, darling. Not now. Not ever.*

"But you deserve to be happy, Elon." Her lush mouth twisted into such a wistful smile that it tugged his heart in every direction at once.

"Thank you, sweetie, but I'm pretty well settled into my single status. Not sure there's much anyone can do to change that." *Except you. And if you're not ready, I'll just keep waiting.*

"We'll see about that." Her reply was so cryptic that it made him smile. "You have a birthday coming up, and I have some brownie points to win back with my best friend. So if I can help make your biggest wish come true..." She let the words settle between them with a soft, secretive smile.

He allowed himself another swift, longing glance at her perfectly curved lips before signaling the waiter to bring him the check. *I'm not holding my breath, sugar, seeing as you still don't have a clue you're the only woman in the world for me.*

The Billionaire's Birthday Blind Date
is available in eBook, paperback, and Kindle Unlimited!

Read the whole trilogy!
The Billionaire's Birthday Date
The Billionaire's Birthday Blind Date
The Billionaire's Birthday Secret

Much love,
Jo

ALSO BY JO

For the most up-to-date printable list of my sweet contemporary books:

Click here

or go to:

https://www.JoGrafford.com/books

For the most up-to-date printable list of my sweet historical books:

Click here

or go to:

https://www.jografford.com/joviegracebooks

ABOUT JO

Jo is an Amazon bestselling author of sweet and inspirational romance stories about faith, hope, love and family drama with a few Texas-sized detours into comedy.

1.) Follow on Amazon!
amazon.com/author/jografford

2.) Join Cuppa Jo Readers!
https://www.facebook.com/groups/CuppaJoReaders

3.) Follow on Bookbub!
https://www.bookbub.com/authors/jo-grafford

4.) Follow on YouTube!
https://www.youtube.com/channel/UC3R1at97Qso6BXiBIx CjQ5w

5.) Follow on Instagram!

https://www.instagram.com/jografford/

amazon.com/authors/jo-grafford

bookbub.com/authors/jo-grafford

facebook.com/jografford

Made in United States
North Haven, CT
05 August 2024